The Healing of Christmas

A Frosty Season Series

Katie Winters

Prologue

Christmas Eve at the Cherry Inn always ended with Grandpa's story. As snow swirled outside the bay windows of the old Victorian home, forming drifts along the street and lining branches of maples and oaks, Grandpa Hank gathered all eight of the Summers' grandchildren around the Christmas tree. They were tired from a long day in the snow, their cheeks ruddy from the cold, their bellies stuffed with Christmas Eve dinner and Grandma Dee's cinnamon cookies. They were the happiest children in the world— sure of the love around them and the approach of Santa Claus, who was surely on his way across the starry night sky.

Grandpa Hank carried the youngest cousin in his strong arms as the rest of them clambered around him, hugging his legs or scrambling to get the best seat on the rug in front of the roaring fire. Grandma Dee followed after them, yet another platter of cookies balanced on her hand, her hair in chaotic curls. "Who wants to hear the

1

story?" Grandpa Hank cried, to which the cousins called, "We do! We do!" Their voices echoed.

"Hank, they'll never sleep if you don't quiet down!" Grandma Dee scolded her husband, her eyes glowing with love.

Charlotte was eight, which put her smack-dab in the middle of her cousins' ages. Shivering with excitement, she sat cross-legged between the Christmas tree and the fireplace, her cheeks warm from the flickering flames and her stomach full after a big Christmas Eve feast. As her cousins quieted down, their parents, the Summers' children, walked in quietly, lining themselves up along the wall. They were adults, but they still found beauty in their father's stories. Their hearts hadn't yet melted.

"Does anyone remember how the story starts?" Grandpa Hank asked, rubbing his gray beard.

"Once upon a time!" Charlotte called triumphantly. She was pleased to be the first to remember.

"That's right, Charlotte. Once upon a time, not so very long ago, a young man met a beautiful young princess," Grandpa Hank went on, his eyes flashing toward Grandma Dee, whose cheeks were flushed. "But the beautiful princess was engaged to a wicked, cruel man who wanted to destroy the Kingdom of Christmas."

"Why would he do that?" Charlotte's younger cousin, Bethany, whispered.

"He wanted to make sure there was no more joy," Grandpa Hank explained. "He wanted to take away presents and candy. He wanted to fire Santa Claus!"

The cousins gasped, just as they did every year. It never got old.

"The young man knew he needed to save the princess from the cruel and wicked man," Grandpa Hank went on.

2

"So he journeyed through the dark forest, where he was forced to fight whatever monsters the wicked man sent for him."

The cousins' eyes glinted with firelight as they watched their grandfather, captivated. Charlotte's heart thumped hard in her chest, and she leaned forward, chin on her fist, watching as her grandfather grew more and more animated as the story progressed— as this young man fought the dragon, the evil reindeer, the toy maker who hated children, all in pursuit of the wicked man and the princess he'd fallen in love with. Throughout, Grandma Dee shook her head, laughed gently, and gazed at Grandpa adoringly, all the way up till the tail-end of the story, when the hero finally defeated the wicked man and saved Christmas.

"After the hero saved Christmas, he asked the beautiful princess to run away with him and get married," Grandpa continued. "He couldn't believe it when she said yes." Here, his eyes locked with Grandma Dee's, and they shared a special, quiet moment as their grandchildren sat rapt with attention between them.

"They traveled far and wide together," Grandpa Hank went on, his voice wavering. "Until they found a gorgeous, abandoned castle in the middle of a small village. Does anyone know what that village was called?"

Charlotte was quick to the draw yet again: "White Plains!" she called.

"That's right." Grandpa Hank smiled lovingly. "They decided this was the castle in which they would live for the rest of their days. They restored the castle with paint and wallpaper; they fixed the hardwood floors, and they even built a beautiful library upstairs so that the beautiful princess could read to her heart's content. After the castle was ready, they began to invite weary travelers to stay the night to rest their weary feet after their journeys through the East. And just two Christmases after that first one, the beautiful princess gave birth to their first child. And they all lived..." He trailed off so the children could cry out: "Happily ever after!"

Charlotte clapped along with her cousins. Grandma Dee cleared the distance between herself and their grandfather and kissed him with her eyes closed. In the chaos of the end of the story, Charlotte hurried back to the cookie platter and selected one shaped like a bell, slathered with frosting. Her cousin, Rudy, who was approximately her age, sidled up beside her and selected a cookie shaped like a reindeer.

"My mom told me that story is based on real life," he announced proudly.

Charlotte's eyes widened. "You mean the evil forest is real?"

Rudy nodded earnestly. "It's the same forest just outside of White Plains!" He lowered his voice even more to add, "And the castle he's talking about? That's the Cherry Inn!"

Although this wasn't entirely a surprise, Charlotte's heartbeat quickened. All her life, she'd considered her grandparents' inn to be the most magical place in the world. There was nothing she loved more than roaming its numerous halls, hiding in its rooms, behind thick curtains and under ornate bed frames, or scouring the books in the upstairs library. If the Cherry Inn was really a castle (which she had to assume was true), then that meant she was pretty close to being a princess, didn't it?

Three days before and after Christmas, Grandpa and Grandma cleared the inn of guests and invited the entire

Summers clan to stay there all together. It was the most magical week of Charlotte's life— a time of dancing, singing, laughing, storytelling, and eating with the people she loved most in the world. Even now, as her aunts and uncles gathered her cousins, preparing them for bed, Charlotte tried to seep up all the memories— to fully remember the soft dough of the cookie and Rudy's silly stories and her grandfather's big laugh. At the age of eight, she'd come to understand that adults just didn't have as much fun as children did, and she'd decided that if she just remembered everything in sharp detail, she would never fall victim to that trap when she got older (if she really ever did become an adult, which seemed unlikely).

Charlotte's mother appeared in the throng of adults and knelt to speak to Charlotte quietly. "How's my big girl? Did you like the story?"

Charlotte's heart swelled with love for her mother. "Rudy says the castle is the Cherry Inn!"

Her mother dropped her chin, and her dark eyes stirred with secrets. "What if I told you the beautiful princess is your grandmother? And the hero is your grandfather?"

Charlotte gazed at her grandma and grandpa, who didn't exactly resemble the princesses and princes in her favorite films and illustrations. Still, she had no reason to refute what her mother told her. Magic sizzled behind her grandma and grandpa's eyes.

Upstairs, Charlotte brushed her teeth and got into bed with her mother. Grandpa and Grandma had given them the Green Room, with its soft wallpaper painted with lush greenery and tiny purple flowers, its green comforter, and its thick green curtains. Her mother fluffed both of their pillows for them and kissed Charlotte on the forehead. "Merry Christmas, my darling."

For a little while, after her mother turned out the light, Charlotte kept her eyes open with excitement. Her ears craned for signs of Santa Claus on the rooftop. Beside her was her mother's profile on the pillow, her eyes closed. For as long as Charlotte could remember, it had just been her and her mother against the world. Kids at school whispered about Charlotte's father, about how he'd left them behind when she'd been very small. Charlotte hadn't yet gotten the nerve to ask her mother about it; she suspected it made her very sad.

But here at the Cherry Inn on Christmas Eve, there was no such thing as sorrow. There was only expectation; there was only the fluffy snow outside, the plump Christmas trees in nearly every room, and the laughter of her cousins, aunts, uncles, and grandparents. Tomorrow morning, Charlotte would awaken to a beautiful Green Room drenched in sunlight. From downstairs would come the smell of cinnamon rolls, bacon, and eggs, and piles of beautifully wrapped presents would encircle the Christmas tree. There was no joy like the joy she felt now, lying in wait for tomorrow morning. And before Charlotte knew it, her eyes were closed, and she plunged into the darkness of her Christmassy dreams.

Chapter One

Present Day

Charlotte tried not to be resentful about how Thanksgiving played out this year. She tried to be rational about it, to remind herself of the facts of her life: she was forty-eight years old; her children were grown and married with responsibilities of their own, and she was divorced. But as she sat at her friend Shonda's Thanksgiving table, surrounded by Shonda's children, husband, siblings, and grandchildren, Charlotte's heart cracked at the edges. She made an excuse before pie and took the train back to her Midtown apartment. The subways were largely empty, with everyone hidden away in their apartments across the city, laughing with their families and eating to their hearts' content. As the sharp wind cracked across her face upon her exit, tears sprang to her eyes.

Shonda had, of course, forced Charlotte to take a few slices of pie back home with her. This left Charlotte in her pajamas with a glass of red wine, watching *Miracle on*

34th Street on television. She remembered what her mother had always said: that *Miracle on 34th Street* wasn't really a Christmas movie; it was a Thanksgiving movie and should be treated as such. "See, Louise? I listened to you. Sometimes." She said this aloud and then filled her mouth with pumpkin pie. She'd once read that being alone and being lonely were two different things, but after growing up surrounded by cousins, aunts, uncles, and grandparents, she'd never been able to differentiate the two.

Charlotte's phone dinged with photographs from her son, Collin. Collin, his wife, Quinn, and their two daughters, Brinlee and Elisa, lived in California— about as far away from New York City as you could get. They were three hours behind, which meant it was only three in the afternoon there. In one photograph, Brinlee and Elisa attempted to eat pumpkin pie, and their cheeks and lips were smeared with purée. In another, Collin carried both of her granddaughters in his arms as Quinn touched his bicep lovingly. Behind them was Quinn's mother, carrying a big turkey on a platter. Charlotte wanted to curse the other woman's luck. She was the grandmother who lived five minutes down the road. She was the one Collin had chosen.

This wasn't entirely Collin's fault, Charlotte knew. Because he was brilliant, he'd gone to grad school in Los Angeles. And because he was a wonderful man, he'd fallen in love. Quinn was born and raised in Los Angeles, and she hadn't wanted to move out east. "She's not used to winter, Mom," Collin had explained. "It would kill her." Charlotte had thought this was a gross exaggeration, but she hadn't said so. Instead, she'd gushed with love for both of them.

Bizarrely, Charlotte hadn't heard from her daughter, Vanessa, yet. Charlotte had texted her that morning to wish her a Happy Thanksgiving and ask how she was feeling. No response. Charlotte returned to their chat and considered pestering her. All things considered, Van was Charlotte's best friend in the world, one of her greatest confidants, and certainly her greatest champion. Unlike her brother, she lived just thirty minutes away with her husband, Grant. And best of all— she was very, very pregnant. She would have the baby any day.

As though Van had sensed Charlotte thinking about her, she called her right that second. Charlotte's heart jumped in her chest, and she answered with a high-pitched, "Happy Thanksgiving!"

"Mom!" Van's voice was strained. "Mom, it's happening."

Charlotte's eyes bugged out. Before she knew what she'd done, she was on her feet, scampering around her living room like a chicken with its head cut off. "Okay. Okay! You've got this, Van," she was saying, as though she were a coach of a softball team. "Are you already at the hospital?"

Van said she was on her way there. "Meet me? Please?"

Charlotte abandoned her pie and wine and sped out the door, where she hailed a taxi and tore across the city to the Brooklyn hospital where Van planned to give birth. All the way there, she shivered so much that her knees clacked together. At a traffic light, she heard herself tell the driver her daughter was having her first baby, and the driver clapped his hands warmly and congratulated her. "A Thanksgiving baby! Isn't that something?"

Once in the hospital, Charlotte made her way to the

labor and delivery hall and discovered Van already in a hospital gown, standing up next to her bed with both of her palms flat across the mattress. She was very pale, and her hair was wild around her face. "Mom!" she cried when she saw her. Charlotte was reminded of when Van had been a little girl, calling out for her after having a nightmare.

"Hey, baby," Charlotte said, wrapping her arms around her. "How are you feeling?"

Charlotte puffed out her cheeks. "Not great," she said simply. Her eyes looked wounded. Charlotte tried to remember her own first delivery twenty-eight years ago when Van had come into the world, yet could think of nothing but pain and terror.

A nurse came in to check on Van, and Charlotte waited by her bed, shifting her weight. All she wanted in the world was to take her daughter's pain away. She held her hand as a contraction came on, and Van's grip threatened to break her bones. But Charlotte told herself her daughter could break all her bones if she needed to. She'd do anything for this grandbaby.

"When did you know today was the day?" Charlotte asked after the nurse left.

Van furrowed her brow. "Around noon, I guess. Ages ago. But the doctor told me not to go to the hospital until the contractions were closer together. I didn't want to just wait around here, killing time, wasting hospital resources."

"Smart," Charlotte said. She had the sudden impulse to tell Van that Van's birth had taken twenty-eight hours but kept her mouth shut. Instead, she asked, "And is Grant on his way?"

Van flared her nostrils and gripped Charlotte's hand

again, preparing for another contraction. Together, they weathered through it as Van gasped for breath and turned a strange shade of reddish purple. Charlotte's stomach twisted in knots of fear. She tried not to think of all the things that could go wrong during labor. It wouldn't do her any good.

After the contraction petered out, Van's chest rose and fell, and she touched her pregnant stomach tenderly. Without looking at her mother, she whispered, "Grant's not coming."

Charlotte was taken aback. "Not coming?"

Van raised her shoulders. "It's okay. I don't want him here, anyway." She said it as though she'd practiced saying it, like a mantra she wanted to remind herself of.

"I thought you were spending Thanksgiving with his family?"

"I was supposed to," Van offered. "But he left three days ago. It would have been pretty strange to show up at his mother's house for Thanksgiving, huh? I'm guessing they didn't put a chair at the table for me."

Charlotte's jaw dropped. Shock rattled through her, and she collapsed on the chair beside her daughter. Leaving your marriage was one thing. But leaving your very pregnant wife? That was something else. That was evil.

It wasn't that Charlotte had ever liked Grant. Van had met him three years ago at a dive bar in Brooklyn when she'd been bartending to put herself through grad school, and Grant had been playing guitar in a psychedelic rock band. Then, as now, Grant had long hair, a beard, and a toned physique and, according to Van, was an up-and-coming celebrity in the music world. Van had fallen head-over-heels with Grant in a way that Charlotte had deemed dangerous. It had all happened so quickly. Before Charlotte had considered what to do about her negative feelings about Grant, he'd moved into Van's apartment and convinced her to take a semester off grad school to cut an album with him. "We're in love, Mom. And it's the best thing in the world," Van had said blissfully over the phone. Charlotte hadn't had the heart to say anything but, "I love you, honey. And I love to see you so happy."

It was clear Van didn't want to talk about Grant, not here in the hospital. As the woman in labor, on the verge of motherhood, she called the shots. Charlotte heard herself coax her through another contraction, then another. When midnight hit, a nurse told them it wouldn't be long now, that she suspected the baby would be born in another hour or so. Van's forehead glistened with sweat as she gaped at the nurse and asked, "Another hour or so?" To Van, it sounded like a death sentence. Charlotte steeled herself for the chaos that came next. The bones of her hand had to be able to take it.

Van's first baby, a boy, was born at one-thirty in the morning on the day after Thanksgiving. Being there beside her darling Van, watching her grandson enter the world, was the third greatest gift of Charlotte's life (after the birth of her own babies, of course). Throughout the drama of the delivery and the soft calm immediately after, Charlotte's heart was shadowed with horrible questions. How could Grant miss the birth of his baby? How could he live with himself?

Not long after Van's baby was born, Charlotte was allowed to hold him. At just seven pounds, he kept his eyes closed, and his fingers and toes wiggled slightly as though he was trying to get used to being out in the air.

He was soft, slightly red, and impossibly adorable. Charlotte's eyes were heavy with tears that she blinked away.

Van was exhausted, as was her right. Not long after the birth, she fell asleep, as did her baby. By contrast, Charlotte felt jumpy and exhilarated, as though it were up to her to remain awake and make sure Van and her baby were safe. It took all her strength to force herself into the hallway and grab a cup of coffee from the vending machine. From there, she paced the waiting room, thinking about her daughter, alone in that moldy Brooklyn apartment with her new baby. That gorgeous, tiny baby. He couldn't live there! It just wouldn't do.

As morning light crept across Brooklyn streets, casting everything in grays and pinks, Charlotte was struck with an idea. Perhaps it was the result of her lack of sleep; perhaps it was absolutely insane. But before she knew what she'd done, she had her phone to her ear, and it was ringing.

It was no surprise that Louise Summers was awake already. At sixty-eight, she got up every morning at four-thirty, did a Pilates workout, and ate a bowl of oatmeal. She was the most regimented woman Charlotte knew.

"Hello?" Louise sounded annoyed.

"Mom. Hi. It's me. It's Charlotte."

Louise made a strange noise in her throat. "What's happened?"

Charlotte leaned against the waiting room wall, her heart pounding. It was true she hadn't called in months. Decades of resentment shimmered in her mother's tone.

"Van had her baby," Charlotte offered.

Louise's voice softened. "Is that so?"

"It's a boy," Charlotte went on, surprised at how

joyful she felt in telling her mother the news. "She did great."

"I'm not surprised. That girl is strong," Louise said.

Charlotte was quiet for a moment. Out on the sidewalk in front of the hospital, a squirrel leaped through the sharp chill of the morning, his belly bulging from overeating before hibernation.

"He doesn't have a name yet," Charlotte continued.

"That will come."

Charlotte sniffed and pressed her forehead against the chill of the window. Fatigue washed over her life in ocean waves, rolling up and back down, so she had the sensation of floating through time.

"Grant left her, Mom. I can't stand it." Charlotte clenched her teeth. "Just days before the birth of his son."

Louise was quiet. Charlotte could feel everything Louise was thinking, her heavy judgment, and she tried not to resent it. There wasn't time for another argument, not now.

"I was wondering," Charlotte went on, "if the Summers family is coming to the Cherry Inn this Christmas? It would be nice to take Van and the baby there. Maybe it would get Van's mind off things here in the city. And you know, Van never spent a Christmas at the Cherry Inn. I've always hated that."

Louise made another noise in her throat, one that Charlotte translated as, *that's your fault, not mine.*

"It would just be nice," Charlotte went on. "Wouldn't it?"

Finally, Louise spoke. "We don't do Christmas at the Cherry Inn anymore. Didn't I tell you that?"

Charlotte's heart skipped a beat. "You didn't mention that."

"Well, it's hard to remember what I've told you and what I haven't," Louise said flippantly.

Charlotte swallowed the lump in her throat. "Maybe I'll call Grandpa and ask him to set aside two rooms for us. It sounds nice to take Van and the baby out of the city for a while."

"The city is no place for a baby," Louise affirmed, which was yet another judgment. Charlotte had raised both of her children in the city. Louise had never approved. "But most of the rooms at the inn aren't suitable for a baby, either."

This surprised Charlotte. "What do you mean?"

"Life has gone on without you here in White Plains, Charlotte," Louise said. "Your grandmother is gone; your grandfather is getting up there. The inn isn't what it used to be."

"I thought Grandpa hired that hotel manager a few years ago? I thought sales were looking up?"

"It's impossible to keep an up-and-coming hotel manager in a tiny place like White Plains," Louise said matter-of-factly. "You should understand that. You left. Remember?"

Charlotte's cheeks burned with a mix of fatigue and shame. For a moment, she stuttered, searching for words.

But then, Louise seemed to break down.

"I'm sure your grandfather is willing to host you, Van, and the new baby in the apartment," she said with a sigh. "Let me go over there this afternoon and talk to him."

Charlotte collapsed in the chair behind her and rubbed her temple. Her mother was firing on all cylinders right now. She felt wrung out.

"Thank you," Charlotte whispered.

"Let me be clear, Charlotte," Louise continued. "I'm

not doing this for you. I'm doing this for Van and the new baby."

"I understand that." Charlotte closed her eyes and wavered in her chair, on the verge of fainting. "I can't thank you enough, anyway. She needs this." *We all do*, she thought.

Chapter Two

The *New York Times* called the exclusive high-rise apartment building on the corner of 104th Street and Manhattan Avenue "Charlie Bryant's Greatest Accomplishment." With sixty-five floors, eight swimming pools, three saunas, two grocery stores, an in-house Apple service station, several gardens with species from forty-four different countries, three movie theaters, and iconic apartment suites promised to film celebrities, it was truly "the place to be," with a waiting list a mile long for Manhattanites wishing to move in.

On December 1st, the apartment building opened its doors to the public for the first time with an incredible Christmas party held in one of the upper-floor ballrooms. Attached to the ballroom were several bars and restaurants, which allowed the guests to feel as though they were on a cruise ship floating over Manhattan.

It was eight-thirty, which meant the party had begun a half-hour ago. Charlie stood in his tuxedo at the window of the apartment he'd decided to live in. It was located on the highest level of the apartment building, towering over the city below, making it seem as though the floor gently swayed beneath him. The swaying was something he would eventually grow accustomed to, he hoped. It was akin to being out at sea.

Twenty floors above the party, Charlie couldn't hear any of its music, its gossip, nor the clacking of utensils as people ate expensive and decadent food. He hadn't been involved in the party planning; he hadn't even wanted to be invited. His tuxedo was altogether too stiff on him, brand-new. A designer had said this was to be his "big step forward" in this Manhattan scene. "You're going to be seen by some of the richest people in Manhattan, all of whom will want to work with you. You need to look the part."

Charlie's assistant, Timothy, texted him, breaking through his reverie.

> TIMOTHY: People are asking about you. Better make an appearance soon, don't you think?

Charlie groaned, shoved his phone back into the pocket of his trousers, and tugged his wild, salt-and-pepper hair, which Timothy had recently suggested he should get cut. Charlie had resented this. It wasn't that he didn't appreciate what Timothy did for him— his guidance, as though Timothy was his mother, ensuring he ate enough protein and got enough sleep. Charlie's career wouldn't have been half what it was without Timothy's clear vision and organizational skills. But more often than not, Charlie wanted to lock himself in his apartment, turn his phone off, let his hair grow long, and fade away from the rest of the world. Timothy wouldn't let him. Charlie's meteoric rise was important to Timothy— especially because Timothy had his sights on becoming a property developer in his own right.

As Charlie entered the party located in the forty-second-floor ballroom, upward of twenty faces flickered toward him, eyes opening wider. The man of the hour had arrived. Charlie touched the breast pocket of his tuxedo nervously but kept his face stoic. He couldn't betray any emotion in front of these people. If he gave them any indication that he was weak, they would eat him alive. That was the nature of Manhattan. Timothy locked eyes with him from the back of the party and gave him a firm nod. The fact that Charlie had decided to show up meant that Timothy was doing his job, keeping Charlie in line. Charlie's stomach twisted into knots.

"Charlie Bryant."

Charlie heard his name and turned slowly. Baxter Bailey, the number one donor for Charlie's iconic building project, strode toward him. Baxter was something of a king across Manhattan. He'd come from old money, which meant he didn't necessarily flaunt it. His singular goal was to be seen as on the cutting-edge of Manhattan society, as being a mover and shaker, apt to alter the course of Manhattan's history.

When Charlie was just thirty-two years old, Baxter had named him his number one property developer, a man through which he planned to strategize his next great maneuvers. Charlie knew that having Baxter as his ally was the single greatest event that had ever occurred in his professional life— one he should be more grateful for. But he'd struggled to feel grateful for anything in many years. Often enough, Timothy had suggested that Charlie thank Baxter more for all he'd done for him. Charlie hadn't bothered.

Charlie and Baxter shook hands. Several photographs were taken by professional photographers hired to showcase the grand opening party. Baxter's teeth were too straight; he was overly botoxed, giving his face an eerie, frozen quality. Yet, despite his seventy-eight years, he was still quite handsome. The date he'd brought to the event that night couldn't have been more than forty. When Timothy had suggested Charlie bring a date for optics reasons, he'd said, "Over my dead body."

"Quite a party, Charlie," Baxter said, dropping his hand after the handshake and trying his best to smile wider. "And quite a building. I think it's your best work yet."

Charlie's cheek twitched. "Couldn't have done it without you, Baxter."

"We both know that's true."

A waiter passed by with a tray of salmon puffs, and Baxter took one and ate it, closing his eyes as he moaned. "These are divine, Charlie. Has anyone told you you're too skinny lately? You have to enjoy the fruits of your labor."

Charlie wasn't hungry; it was rare he was hungry. Far behind Baxter, Timothy waved his hands and mouthed, "eat," and Charlie took a puff and forced himself to chew and swallow it. Of course, it was exquisite, probably the finest-tasting thing in all of Manhattan right now. He didn't care.

"I heard a rumor we're neighbors, Charlie," Baxter said. "Just down the hall from one another."

This hit Charlie hard. "You're moving in?"

"Why wouldn't I want to move into the best apartment building in Manhattan?" Baxter said, spreading his arms out on either side of him. Several journalists around them pressed record on their phones.

"Tell us what it's like to be neighbors with the great Baxter Bailey!" one of them called.

Charlie gritted his teeth. He knew he needed to stroke Baxter's ego in front of these people. He also knew the journalists and the photographers were just there to do their jobs, just as he was. He felt as though they were all in the midst of a video game, each of them given a part to play. Perhaps whoever operated the game was in a basement somewhere, eating Cheetos, trying to get Charlie up to the next level in the game. But what was that level? Putting another building in Manhattan? Creating another beautiful world for rich people who already have everything?

"If you'll excuse me," Charlie said to Baxter. He cut around him and strode across the ballroom. In the corner, the string quintet played a Chopin song he'd loved as a teenager, back when his mother had demanded he study music. She'd been a professional opera singer who'd given up her career after Charlie's father had dragged them to Chicago. Turns out, not many people enjoyed opera in the Midwest. His earliest memories involved her singing in the shower, her voice rising higher and higher until he'd been sure the windows would crack, just as they did in cartoons.

Charlie went upstairs to the attached restaurant, with its view overlooking the ballroom. There, the bartender hurried to stir him up a Dark and Stormy cocktail, his favorite. Charlie hated the way the bartender worked so diligently, as though he worried Charlie would yell at him for not making his cocktail quickly enough. Charlie thanked the bartender and tipped him well, then turned back to oversee the ballroom. But there before him was yet another donor, Marcia Lacey, who grabbed his bicep and gushed about the beautiful building.

"Can you imagine Manhattanites one hundred years from now?" she said. "They're going to pass by and think about us, you know? They're going to know that we changed the history of this city."

Charlie wanted to protest. He wanted to tell her that nobody would think about them in the next few decades, that these people in the future would stride (or fly, what did he know?) past the building, thinking about their own schedules and their relationships and their future dreams. By then, the building would be planted into the texture of New York City. Perhaps people would love it in the same way they loved a tree or a bush. It was just there.

Over and over again throughout the next hour, Charlie was forced into conversations that alternated between utterly banal and infuriating. He was forced to stand in photographs with donors, to sit at tables with the Manhattan elite, and to eat snacks he didn't want. And worst of all, he had no interest in drinking. After one Dark and Stormy, he realized fogging up his reality made him even more alienated from himself. He didn't want to watch himself from a distance. He wanted to be front and center, watching his rage burn brighter.

And suddenly, he heard himself say: "I'm going to get out of the city for a while."

He was in the ballroom again, talking to, of all people, Baxter Bailey. He wasn't entirely sure how he'd gotten there; he couldn't chart the course from the bar to the restaurant back to the ballroom. It was a blur of terrible conversations.

Baxter snapped his hand across Charlie's shoulder and said, "You have another project cooking up, don't you? I should have known that you wouldn't linger for long without anything to do. You're a worker. Like me. I like that in a man."

Charlie didn't care what Baxter thought. He locked eyes with him and gave a firm nod.

"I'll be in touch," Baxter said.

Charlie used Baxter's assumption as fuel. He walked out of the ballroom, pressed his finger to the elevator button, and returned to his apartment. There, he changed out of his tuxedo, then threw jeans, sweatshirts, flannels, socks, and underwear into a large backpack, one he'd meant to use to hike the Himalayas. He and Sarah had been planning that for years.

When he left his apartment, he didn't even bother to glance back at it. It held no semblance of him. It was an empty shell.

In the elevator on the way down to the garage level, Charlie looked for cabin rentals online. He imagined himself deep in the woods somewhere, with a wood-burning stove, a thick beard, and a red flannel shirt like a lumberjack. The whole nine yards. He imagined what Sarah would say about that: that he was milking his loneliness. Maybe he was. But it was better than living in a gorgeous apartment in the sky. He wanted to be amongst the trees again. He wanted to breathe real air.

By the time he reached his car (a Porsche, which he now felt was ostentatious), Charlie found the cabin. It was situated a few miles outside of a quaint village in New Jersey, shrouded with trees. Past reviewers said wildlife like rabbits, deer, skunks, and even beavers could be seen from the back window, cutting through the woods to get wherever they were going. It had been ages since Charlie had seen an animal besides a New York City rat.

Just his luck, in booking the cabin, he learned there was a keypad out front. This meant Charlie just had to insert the code, and the key would pop out. He didn't have to speak to anyone.

As Charlie waited in the garage entrance, his hands at ten and two as street traffic cleared, his speaker system spoke to him.

"Text from Timothy," a woman's computerized voice said. "It says: 'Charlie, where are you? Baxter is saying something about another development somewhere. Outside the city? Remember, I can't help you unless you clue me in a little on your plans!'"

But Charlie didn't have the energy to text Timothy back. He hoped Timothy would consider this a well-earned vacation. He would still be paid handsomely; Charlie would even send him an enormous Christmas bonus.

But Charlie had no interest in sharing news of where he was with anyone. He wanted to hide himself away; he wanted to forget his own name.

"Text Timothy back," he said to his device. "Timothy. Take December off. Go home. Be with your wife and children. In January, I'll be in contact about the next step of your career. You don't want to be an assistant for the rest of your life. I know that, and you know that." He paused and slammed his foot on the gas to get out of the garage and drive out onto the street. Although he didn't cut anyone off, another driver blared his horn— presumably because everyone in New York City was just in a bad mood all the time. "Remember to take the time to be with your family as much as you can," Charlie added in his text to Timothy. "You don't know how long you have."

Chapter Three

Van named her baby Ethan. For the first week of Ethan's life, Van, Charlotte, and Ethan lived in Charlotte's apartment in Midtown. They hardly left, ordering groceries to the apartment door, taking shifts to care for the baby, and packing their bags for their big trip to White Plains. They'd decided to leave on December 2nd when Ethan was a full week old.

Although she never would have admitted it to Van, it didn't surprise Charlotte that Grant hadn't reached out since the birth. He was that sort of man, apt to run away from responsibility the minute things got tough. Van was doubled over with a mix of all-encompassing love for her baby and grief for her failed marriage, an onslaught of emotions that often kept her awake all hours of the night. Charlotte didn't know what to do. As her daughter wept in her arms, she considered driving to wherever Grant was staying and knocking on his door until he answered. At that point, what? Would she scream at him? Threaten him? Demand he come back? Her fantasy always ended there.

One thing she had to do before they left the city was retrieve Van's baby supplies from the apartment she'd shared with Grant. Because Van was too exhausted to go herself, Charlotte slotted the key into the door and crept through the apartment, feeling as though she'd broken in. Just as Van had told her, all of Ethan's baby supplies were in the nursery. Before she loaded it in the trunk of her car downstairs, she went through the rest of the house, trying to imagine what had gone wrong in her daughter's marriage. There was a photograph of the couple on their wedding day hanging on the wall. Another photograph of Van and Charlotte from that day was perched on the table by the window. There was a photograph of Van, her brother, and his daughters on the dresser in the bedroom. Van's clothing still hung in the closet and was folded in drawers. It seemed that Grant had come by at some point and taken anything he wanted— a pair of keys sat on the kitchen table, glinting expectantly. This was more proof he wanted out for good.

"Coward," Charlotte said to the keys. She felt crippled with a sense of dread.

But on the morning of December 2nd, Charlotte slotted the final suitcase into the back of her car and watched as Van clicked Ethan's baby car seat into place. Her heart thrummed with expectation. If there was one thing she could count on, it was the Cherry Inn.

In the passenger seat, Van sipped her coffee and fiddled with the radio stations. Charlotte drove slowly through the garage nearest her apartment building and waited as the lever raised between the lot and the street, freeing her.

"Getting out of the city always makes me feel like an

animal escaping the zoo," she joked as she dropped the wheels from the curb and onto the road.

Van laughed, and the sound of it opened Charlotte's heart. When she glanced at her daughter, she saw a young woman with large circles under her eyes and her hair unkempt. There was a small stain on the front of her shirt. But none of that mattered. Once they reached White Plains, everything would be easier. And Grandpa Hank's love would smother them. With a newborn in tow, there was no such thing as too much love.

"I was trying to remember the last time I was in White Plains," Van said. "It must have been fifteen or sixteen years ago?"

Charlotte's heart thudded. Had it really been that long?

"I think I was twelve," Van went on. "Collin was ten or so. It was summer, and we spent two weeks at the Cherry Inn. Great-Grandpa taught us to play Rummy and let us roam downtown by ourselves. Coming from the city, it felt crazy to be without an adult. I remember thinking it was the most magical place in the world. Collin and I daydreamed about moving there."

"Did you?"

Van nodded and furrowed her brow. "Don't get me wrong, Mom. We loved being city kids. We had our finger on the pulse of everything. We were happy. It's just that White Plains felt like freedom to us. I'm sure it didn't feel the same for you. Especially with Grandma around the corner."

Charlotte tried to visualize her children at twelve and ten— and herself at thirty-two. By that time, she'd been a single mother for several years, making her life up as she went along. She was pretty sure she'd gotten almost everything wrong.

Had her children been able to sense Charlotte's resentment toward her own mother over the years? How often did she talk about it? Her cheeks were flushed with embarrassment.

After the argument with Louise that had changed everything, Charlotte wanted to take herself out of the equation. She'd kept a wide berth, coming to White Plains only in the summertime and then not at all. She'd been so stubborn.

The drive from the city to White Plains took approximately two hours. Throughout, Ethan slept wonderfully, his little hand curled around the strap of his car seat. Van turned around quickly every few minutes to check on him, craning her neck.

"I can't believe how perfect he is," Van whispered several times. "Even just a few months ago, I was freaking out about how I was going to manage motherhood."

"But it came naturally to you," Charlotte offered gently. "Didn't it?"

"Not everything," Van admitted, settling back in the passenger seat and crossing her arms. "But I'm starting to understand the concept of 'mother's intuition.' It's sort of magical, isn't it?"

Charlotte nodded and swallowed the lump in her throat. She remembered that feeling more than anything, the sudden realization that everything she'd once understood about the world was incorrect or didn't matter anymore.

The sign for White Plains appeared on the righthand side of the highway. Van clapped her hands quietly and said, "Here we are! Our Christmas home!" They hadn't yet discussed what they would do after Christmas was over. Charlotte decided they'd cross that bridge when they came to it.

The Cherry Inn was located on Main Street. Built in 1843, it featured Victorian architecture, adorable lace-like eaves, slanted rooftops, ornate window shutters, big porches in the back and front, and ten suites, complete with bathrooms. Back in the nineties, it had been the subject of several travel television shows, in which travel writers stayed over and spoke about the beautiful architecture of the house and the coziness of White Plains.

Charlotte parked the car out front and cut the engine. Just as always, the Cherry Inn towered over them, shrouded with oaks and maples, their limbs twisting toward a sky heavy with gray clouds. As they gazed at the old inn, the clouds burst open, and soft fluffs of snow began to fall to the brown grass below.

"It looks different than I remember," Van offered tentatively.

Charlotte's throat felt tight, and she rubbed it, peering closer at the house. It was true that it needed more than a coat of paint. Several of the shutters had fallen off, and the swing on the front porch was unattached and rotting on the porch floor. A window upstairs was cracked, and all the flower beds in the front looked as though they'd been dug up years ago.

"Your grandma said the suites aren't ready for guests," Charlotte offered. "But we're staying in the back apartment with your great-grandfather."

Van's chin quivered. "Why do you think it got so bad?"

"I don't know." Charlotte tugged her hair nervously. "Your great-grandfather is eighty-eight."

"And Great-Grandma has been gone a long time," Van said quietly.

In the back seat, Ethan gurgled and then let out a loud cry. Van hopped to it, shoving herself into the passenger door and hurrying to get Ethan out of his car seat. "I need to feed him," she announced. "You ready to go in?"

Because Ethan needed to be fed immediately, Charlotte and Van left the bags in the car and walked up the porch steps. Just like always, there was a key under the welcome mat for the front door, and Charlotte opened it and led Van through the shadows of the old place. It looked as though nobody had walked through the foyer in many years. The front desk, mahogany and once ornate and glowing, was heavy with dust. Most of the furniture had been covered with white sheets, and the fireplace was filled with a pile of ash. The walls were badly in need of paint or fresh wallpaper.

It was hard to believe this was where the Summers family had had their joyous Christmas parties— that here, the Summers cousins had gathered around Grandpa Hank, begging him for his Christmas Eve story. If Charlotte closed her eyes for a split-second and forced herself deep into her memories, she could just-barely imagine the smell of baking Christmas cookies, the laughter of her grandmother, and her grandfather's voice, imparting the magical story of his life. Very early on in her life, she'd understood that Grandpa Hank had chosen to tell that story every year to prove to his wife just how much he loved and still loved her. It was far more romantic than anything Charlotte's ex-husband had ever done for her.

"Let's just go through the kitchen," Charlotte said to Van, guiding her through the dust-filled kitchen, where another series of doors led her to the entrance of the apartment. It was here that Grandpa Hank and Grandma Dee had raised their children, never far from the demands of the inn.

Charlotte knocked on the apartment door, suddenly petrified. It felt as though she'd entered a haunted house. Although her mother had said the apartment was ready for them, Charlotte was terrified that the door would open to reveal a dusty apartment with busted cupboards and cracked windows. Perhaps everything she'd left behind in White Plains was broken.

But a moment later, the door opened. Grandpa Hank stood before them, still just under six feet tall despite his age, wearing a navy blue knitted sweater and a pair of slacks. Sleepily, he rubbed his eyes, and his face broke into an enormous smile.

"My darling girls!" he called. "You made it!" Charlotte had never heard a more nourishing sound than his voice. Grandpa Hank gathered them in his arms, careful not to fuss the baby. "And this must be my newest great-great grandchild?" He bent to touch Ethan's hand tenderly with the tip of his finger. His eyes glinted with tears. "You've been on the planet just a few days, little pal. Stick with me. I'll show you the ropes."

Van laughed. "It's so good to see you, Great-Grandpa."

"And you, beautiful Van! You're a new mother! What a wonderful thing!"

Van stepped around Grandpa Hank, adjusting Ethan in her arms. "He needs to be fed," she explained.

"Your bedrooms are all ready," Grandpa Hank said, beckoning for Charlotte to enter so he could close the door behind her. "Yours is the first door on the right, Van. And Charlotte, I gave you your mother's old room."

As Van disappeared into her bedroom to nurse Ethan, Charlotte gave her grandfather another hug. The last time she'd seen him was four years ago when he'd come into the city with her cousin, Rudy. They'd attended one of her book readings, sitting in the audience dutifully until the question-and-answer session. At that point, her grandfather had waved his hand in the air like a child and asked, "How did you get so brilliant, Charlotte Summers?" Charlotte laughed and explained to the audience, "That's just my grandfather. Nobody else thinks I'm brilliant. Not even my mother!" The audience had laughed.

"Sit down," her grandfather instructed. He ambled to his La-Z-Boy and dropped himself delicately onto the cushion. Charlotte grabbed the couch across from him. On television, he watched *Law and Order*, but the volume was turned way down, and the subtitles were on. When Hank caught her looking, he waved his hand and said, "I hate hearing too many voices this early in the day."

Charlotte laughed. He seemed just the same as ever. Behind him was a hanging portrait of him and Grandma Dee on their wedding day sixty-eight years ago. Her grandmother's face was captivated, proof of her tremendous love for him. It felt impossible that she'd been taken from the world so many years ago. Grandpa Hank had never even tried to find love again.

"Can't believe Grant left our girl," Grandpa Hank grumbled, his eyes darkening. "Right in her time of need."

Charlotte rubbed the back of her neck. She wondered if her grandfather and mother had had a similar conversation when her ex had left her. Probably.

"But she's with us now," Grandpa Hank went on. "We'll protect her."

Charlotte wet her lips. She considered the shadowy, busted inn attached to the apartment, a space that had once been her grandfather's pride and joy. Should she ask him what went wrong? When he'd closed down the inn? Why he'd given up?

"We'll have to get a Christmas tree," Grandpa Hank added. "It's baby Ethan's first Christmas. And that means something. I won't let him down."

Charlotte reached across the living room and took her grandfather's hand— which was large and heavy with wrinkles, the knuckles round. These hands had done so much— they'd put up the shutters around the inn windows, prepared sandwiches for grandchildren, held babies, and driven cars safely home. For a moment, Charlotte and Grandpa Hank locked eyes with one another, and Charlotte dropped through thousands of memories.

"I feel old, Grandpa," Charlotte said quietly.

"If you're old, what does that make me?" Grandpa Hank said with a laugh.

Charlotte squeezed his hand and sighed. It was her first Christmas back at the Cherry Inn in twenty-eight years, and she planned to make the most of it. Her grandfather was right; they had to do it for baby Ethan. Despite past resentments and so many mistakes, they had to show him what the Summers family was all about. A baby was a new start. A baby was hope.

Chapter Four

The cabin on the outskirts of White Plains featured a queen-sized bed, a wood-burning fireplace, a jagged counter that looked straight from *Little House on the Prairie*, an ax, presumably for cutting trees, and an empty refrigerator. It couldn't have been further from the high-rise apartment building Charlie had just developed in Manhattan. The people who'd just been at the opening party, demanding Charlie's attention, would have been scandalized. Why would the sought-after property developer, Charlie Bryant, choose to live out his holidays here?

When Charlie awoke at the cabin after a heavy night of sleep, his stomach gurgled with hunger, and he rolled over and blinked around him, trying to make sense of his surroundings. In a flash, it all came back to him: his wild drive through the night, pulling up next to the cabin at three in the morning, removing the keys from the safe, and collapsing on the bed. He rose and leaned against the headboard, rubbing his eyes of sleep. New York City now seemed like a nightmare, a collection of people who demanded his attention, his energy, his time at every turn. He wanted to be a different person. He wanted to start over.

But first, Charlie needed coffee. As the cabin hadn't been equipped with anything, he had to head to town.

Charlie emerged from the cabin and into the crisp light of the morning. He was still in his sweatpants and a sweatshirt, an outfit he never would have allowed himself in the city, and he slid into the front seat of his car before checking the map and realizing he was only about a mile away from town. It just so happened there was a trail through the woods to get to the nearest grocery store. Abandoning his Porsche, he hiked the woods, his chin raised as flashes of sunlight dropped through the treetops. He heard nothing but the twitter of winter birds and smelled nothing but the soft soil and the trees. The contrast to Manhattan was night and day.

Eventually, the forest cleared and left him at the outer edge of White Plains, an adorable village with an old-world Main Street peppered with Victorian houses, an ancient-looking movie theater, several churches, their steeples glinting in the bright blue sky, and a little grocery store. He entered the store and found himself in a mom-and-pop shop with no more than three aisles, locally-made bread in the little bakery, fresh fruits and vegetables, and only one or two types of everything else— from cereal to crackers to soups. Charlie grabbed a package of coffee, some cans of soup, crackers, tuna, cheese, and bread for sandwiches. He wanted the simplicity of a different life. He never wanted to eat another three-hundred-dollar meal of tapas ever again.

Charlie paid a very low price for a big paper bag of food, then stood on Main Street for a little while, eating a crisp apple and looking at everything. Several locals passed by as he ate, waving happily. They wore sweaters with Christmas patterns, and their smiles were genuine, even as their eyes questioned who he might be. This seemed the sort of town where everyone knew everyone, where gossip flowed freely. That was okay. Charlie had bought enough supplies to live off of coffee, sandwiches, and soup for about a week. He would only emerge from his cabin when he had to.

As Charlie ate his apple, he couldn't help but notice the state of several of the old Victorian homes on Main Street. It wasn't hard to imagine how they'd once been, stately and proud, pastel colors, several of them with three floors and sharp rooftops. But now, many of them were dilapidated. Their front porches were crumbling, missing shutters, and needed paint. One of them in particular looked on the brink of collapse. A rusty sign out front read: The Cherry Inn.

Charlie's over-active developer imagination kick-started. If only someone could swoop into White Plains and flip these gorgeous houses. He could do it, of course. He knew how.

But no. He shook his head and turned back toward the cabin, tossing his apple core in a nearby trash can. He'd come to White Plains to get away from thoughts like these. He'd come to meditate on his life, to make peace with himself, and to decide what was next for him. Perhaps he would never develop another property again.

After another hike through the woods, Charlie returned to his cabin and made a fire in the fireplace. Afterward, he made a melted ham and cheese sandwich and read a book for several hours, getting up every once in a while to add another log to the fire. He hadn't had his cell phone on since he'd arrived, and he took pleasure in imagining Timothy or Baxter Bailey trying to call him. He'd abandoned his life. He'd become a ghost. He was thrilled.

The next day and the one after that, Charlie kept up the same schedule. He read by the fire, took walks through the woods, ate sandwiches, and watched the snowfall from the windows. His phone remained off. His connection to the outside world was dead. And he hadn't heard himself speak aloud since he'd thanked the grocery clerk, a fact that pleased him. He hadn't realized how much he'd grown to hate himself until now. Maybe he could take a vow of silence. Maybe he could move to Asia and become a Buddhist.

But on the third day, Charlie woke up with a horrible heaviness in his chest. He'd been plagued with nightmares for hours, and images and sounds crashed through his mind: flashing lights and screams. He couldn't stop his racing heart. Not even reading or walking through the woods calmed him.

As dusk draped itself over the woods, Charlie donned his winter coat, hat, and gloves and trudged back into the woods. He kept his eyes on the ground, and he tried to focus on his breathing. But every few minutes, the same fear and dread returned, and he staggered forward, gripped the side of a tree, and sputtered with sorrow.

He now remembered why he'd kept himself busy for so many years, with scarcely a day off. All that work had kept his demons at bay. He'd forgotten.

When Charlie reached White Plains again, he heard music coming from a road just beyond Main Street, and he went toward it like a moth to a flame. Overhead, twinkling lights had been strung from one side of the street to the other, and garlands and wreaths hung from business doors. A sign that read: "Merry Christmas, White Plains!" was featured on the front lawn of the courthouse, along with a nativity scene. It was clear that whoever oversaw Christmas decor in White Plains took her job very seriously.

The music was coming from a bar on the corner called Rudy's. Charlie rubbed his temples, thinking that a Dark and Stormy might do him good. Out in front of the bar, two older men smoked cigars and gossiped with one another, their cheeks bright red from cold.

"Hi there," one of them said as Charlie approached. "You aren't from around here."

Charlie stopped short and grimaced into a smile. "I'm not, no."

The men smiled at him curiously. It seemed they had nothing better to do than smoke cigars on the front patio of a dive bar, waiting for strangers to pass by. Perhaps they'd been doing that for thirty-plus years.

"Where you from?" the other guy asked.

"I was born in Chicago."

"Chicago! The Windy City!" They smiled wider as the one on the right asked, "And what brings you here? You got family here?"

Charlie wanted to tell the men to mind their own business— but he knew that gossip traveled quickly in a town like this, and he didn't want any trouble with the locals. As soon as his dread went away, he wanted to return to the cabin, read his books, eat his sandwiches, and enjoy his solitude.

"I'm up the road in a cabin," Charlie said. "I wanted to get away from the city for a while."

"The Marshall Cabin?"

"Yes," Charlie said, remembering the sign that hung out front.

"You're all on your own out there?" the other asked, his lips parted.

"I prefer it that way," Charlie assured them, rubbing his palms together. Somehow, in pretending to be kind to them when he didn't want to, a surge of goodwill toward the men came over him. It was the same as faking it till he made it, he supposed. "I'll see you in there?"

Charlie entered the warmth of the bar, which had a square-shaped counter in the center and fifteen or so wooden tables scattered throughout. Hanging above the bar were silent televisions showing sporting events as well as a local spelling bee. Christmas lights were strung throughout, and a Christmas tree glowed in the corner, its star brighter than the Empire State Building.

"Evening!" The bartender behind the counter planted a large beer in front of a local who sat at the counter and stared at the spelling bee.

"Hey." Charlie felt all twenty pairs of eyes in the bar turn toward him and size him up. His head still throbbing from his strange day, he forced himself to the bar, sat down, and said, "Can I get a Dark and Stormy?"

The bartender's eyes glinted with intrigue. "Now that's a drink people around here don't order so often."

Charlie felt as though he had a target on his back. Everywhere he went, he was seen as this swanky city man, which couldn't have been further from how he really felt. In his heart and soul, he was still that Chicago kid who'd come from nothing, whose mother had sung opera in the shower, nursing her broken heart after her failed career.

"Here you are." The bartender placed the drink in

front of him and then leaned against the counter, his eyes on the inky sky outside.

Charlie took a small sip of his drink, expecting it to be subpar. After all, he was in a dive bar in the middle of nowhere— nothing compared to the five-star bars he frequented back in Manhattan. But the ginger beer, dark rum, and lime came together in a perfect balance. Had Baxter Bailey been there, he would have called the drink "exquisite."

"Wow," Charlie said before he could stop himself. "This is really good."

The bartender brightened. "You think? I haven't made one in years."

Charlie was charmed by the bartender's surprise. "I've had thousands of these over the years. This must be the best one."

The bartender's smile widened. "I should record you saying that. I want to show off to my friends later." The bartender stood up straight and extended his hand. "My name is Rudy, by the way."

Charlie remembered that the bar itself was named Rudy's. "I'm Charlie," he said. Already, he found that the pressure on his chest had loosened, and his lungs were filling with air. He took another sip of his cocktail, noting that Rudy continued to look at him curiously.

"You're not from around here," Rudy said. "Not that it's any of my business."

"I'm not," Charlie said. "I grew up in Chicago, but I live in Manhattan."

"And what brings you out here?"

Charlie raised his shoulders. How could he translate the current horrors of his life to a bartender in a small town?

"I'm being nosy," Rudy said with a laugh. "Just ignore me."

Suddenly, the bar door flung open, bringing with it a sharp, cold draft. Rudy's face shifted, and he scrambled out from behind the bar to swallow someone in a hug. Against Charlie's better judgment, he kept his eyes upon Rudy, listening as Rudy cried out, "I heard you were around! What the heck took you so long?" Clearly, the woman he hugged wasn't his wife or girlfriend. Who was she?

It didn't matter, Charlie reminded himself, forcing his eyes back to his drink. He was miles away from the city, drinking his cocktail. Nobody here cared about him beyond their curiosity. Up above him, on the television showing the spelling bee, a kid no older than ten successfully spelled "milquetoast," a word Charlie had never even heard of before. Sarah would have known that word. She would have spelled it successfully. He took another long drink and faded away from himself for a moment, listening to the chords of the song coming from the speakers and the humming conversation between Rudy and the woman who'd just entered the bar. He felt like a ghost haunting the bar.

Rudy appeared on the other side of the counter again, his hands on his hips as he chatted with the newcomer. The woman who'd entered picked a stool two away from Charlie, removing her coat and leaping up onto the chair as though she were twenty-something. Upon closer inspection, Charlie decided she wasn't much younger than him, with big, dark eyes like a puppy dog's, thick dark hair, and a smile that lit up the bar. She looked captivated by Rudy.

"Just a white wine? You don't want something fancier?" Rudy was asking her. "This gentleman over here ordered a Dark and Stormy."

For the first time, the woman at the counter turned and arched her eyebrow in Charlie's direction. "I haven't had one of those in years."

"And I hadn't made one in years," Rudy said. "But Charlie here says it's the best he's ever had."

Under intense scrutiny from this woman, Charlie blushed and raised his drink nervously. "It's really good."

The woman rapped her knuckles on the counter. "One Dark and Stormy, Rudy. Thanks."

As Rudy stirred up the cocktail, he said, "This is my cousin, Charlotte. She just got into White Plains from the city, too."

Charlie decided Charlotte could be yet another distraction as he chased his fears away at this bar. After a slow nod, he said, "Manhattan?"

"Midtown," she said. "You?"

"Upper West Side."

Normally, when Charlie said he lived in the Upper West Side, people made a fuss. It was clear he had money. Charlotte's eyes didn't even sparkle with recognition. It was as though he'd said he lived in Ohio.

"I hope you enjoy White Plains," Charlotte said with a last smile before returning her eyes to Rudy.

That was it. The cold shoulder. Charlie reminded himself he hadn't wanted any company at all, that he'd just come into town for a drink. He took another sip and returned his attention to the spelling bee, where a little girl even younger than the last kid spelled "conscientiousness." Even still, he couldn't help but eavesdrop on Rudy and Charlotte. They were right beside him, after all.

"I can't believe Aunt Louise didn't mention you were

coming to town," Rudy was saying to Charlotte as he placed the drink in front of her. "She was just in here the other day."

"You know Mom doesn't like to talk about me," Charlotte said.

Rudy sighed. "How long has it been since the fight?"

"More than twenty-eight years."

Rudy's cackle was somber. "You and Louise are just about the most stubborn women I know. And I own a bar. I see a lot of stubbornness come through here." He was quiet for a moment. "But you reached out to her first?"

Charlotte raised her shoulders. "I panicked after my grandson was born. He was just so small! You always forget how small they are on that first day. Nostalgia took over. All I wanted was to take Van and baby Ethan home to the Cherry Inn. I wanted them to experience Christmas the way we always did back in the seventies and eighties."

"Before your fight with your mother, you mean."

"Of course."

Rudy palmed the back of his neck. "It must have been a surprise for you, seeing the Cherry Inn like that."

"It's awful," Charlotte agreed. "It looks like a haunted house."

"I tried to help out where I could," Rudy said. "But Grandpa just couldn't bring in the same customer base. He tried social media for a while, but that was a bust. Money was not flowing through there anymore. Eventually, my parents and Aunt Louise advised him to stop advertising the inn altogether and live off his savings. And now, so much time has passed." He trailed off.

"It was probably a good call," Charlotte said reticently. "But it breaks my heart. Remember how magical it looked at Christmas?"

"I hate thinking about it," Rudy said.

"Van and I are staying in the apartment out back with Grandpa. It's much more comfortable than either of our apartments in the city. Much bigger if you can believe it," Charlotte went on. "But I think, after Christmastime, we should consider selling the old place. Maybe Grandpa would want to move into a retirement home."

"It'll be hard to get him to leave that inn," Rudy said. "You remember the old story."

"The hero and his princess?" Charlotte said with a soft smile. "I could never forget it."

Rudy laughed. "Right. Of course. That story changed your life. I forgot."

Charlotte took a long drink from her Dark and Stormy. Charlie couldn't take his eyes away, and his heart raced. And then, for reasons Charlie would never understand, he asked, "Excuse me?"

Charlotte and Rudy turned and blinked at Charlie.

"Are you talking about one of the Victorian homes on Main Street? The one that looks so broken down?"

Charlotte's face crumpled. "The Cherry Inn. Our grandfather opened it sixty-five years ago."

"Do you have a photograph of what it used to look like?" Charlie's heartbeat quickened. What was he doing?

Charlotte removed her phone from her purse and flicked through her photographs to find an old photograph of the inn in its former glory. It had been painted a soft lilac color, and it looked like something out of a book of fairy tales. On the front porch in the photograph, a middle-aged woman raised her hand to wave at whoever took the picture.

"That's my Grandma Dee," Charlotte said. "She must have been about fifty there. I'm nearly fifty now. Isn't that strange?"

Charlie shifted on his stool. As he gazed at the woman in the photograph, dressed in eighties fashion, he was reminded of his own mother back in Chicago, waving to him from the window of their apartment building as he'd headed to school.

"You know what?" Charlie began, his mouth suddenly dry. "I'm actually a property developer."

Charlotte looked at him with big eyes as though she were suddenly frightened of him.

"What does a property developer do?" Rudy asked.

Charlie wanted to laugh. In Manhattan, everyone knew what a property developer did. "Basically, I'm responsible for all sorts of building projects. I make it so new buildings are built, and old buildings are renovated."

"And then, you turn them for a profit," Charlotte said nervously.

"But in this case, I would just help you renovate," Charlie said. "And then, you could do whatever you want."

"But you'd want a fee," Charlotte pointed out.

"Of course," Rudy said, nodding.

"Nothing major," Charlie said. "We could work that out after it's done."

Charlotte continued to look at him distrustfully. Charlie understood. Why would this Manhattanite swoop into White Plains and do a good deed like this for very little money? It didn't make any sense.

But to explain his reasons to her, he'd have to reveal

the devastation of his aching heart. And he never spoke about that to anyone.

He just wanted to do something good in the world. He wanted to work on a project that actually mattered— one that had nothing to do with Manhattan millionaires.

"We can talk about it," Charlotte said, furrowing her brow. "But you can back out at any time."

"We would understand if it was too much work," Rudy assured him. "The inn means a lot to us. But it's just our memories, you know? It's hard to explain to an outsider."

"Just let me take a look at the place," Charlie urged. "Maybe it's not as bad as you think it is. It's hard to tell. Maybe it's just a quick fix."

Chapter Five

Christmas 1995

The front door of the Cherry Inn burst open before Charlotte had a chance to knock. Immediately, she was blown over with hugs from her cousin, Bethany, her Grandma Dee, her cousin, Rudy, her Aunt Tina, her Grandpa Hank, and finally, her mother, Louise, who wrapped her in an embrace so strong that Charlotte couldn't breathe for a moment. When she was released, Louise placed her hands on either side of Charlotte's face and whispered, "I missed you so much."

It was true that Charlotte and Louise hadn't seen one another in several months. This was a rarity for them; perhaps it was the longest they'd ever gone. Charlotte knew this was her fault. She'd run off to college in New York City and thrown herself completely into her creative writing and art classes. She'd decided she would make something of herself someday—that she'd write and illustrate her own children's books and travel the world telling people her stories.

The secret she'd come to tell her mother burned within her. It took all her strength not to blurt it out now as Louise beckoned Charlotte inside and closed the door firmly behind her, securing them in the warmth of the Cherry Inn.

"This place never changes," Charlotte said as she unraveled her scarf from her neck.

"Did you want it to?" Louise asked.

"Never!" Charlotte said with a laugh. How could she explain the truth to her mother? Whenever she was anxious, petering on the brink of insanity in the city, she always closed her eyes and imagined herself to be eight years old, seated in front of the Christmas tree at the Cherry Inn. She imagined time hadn't had its way with her and scooped her into the modern age.

"Good," Louise said with a smile. "We don't want you to change, either."

Charlotte followed Louise past the front desk and into the living room. Just like every other Christmas, her Grandma and Grandpa had stopped accepting guests for the week before and after Christmas and cleared the suites for only their children and grandchildren. The Christmas tree was overwhelmingly thick, its branches reaching out half-way across the living room, and beneath it were piles of beautifully wrapped presents. Although Charlotte was now twenty years old, she allowed herself a moment of childlike wonder. She closed her eyes and inhaled the smells of cinnamon, pine, and crumbling wood in the fire.

Grandpa Hank and Grandma Dee emerged from the kitchen with platters of Christmas cookies.

"Come now! Eat up! Let me do my grandmotherly

duty," Grandma Dee said, drawing a platter toward Charlotte.

Charlotte laughed and took a cut-out of a star. "You spoil us, Grandma."

"What else is a grandmother for?" Grandma Dee asked, flitting around the living room to deliver more cookies.

Charlotte glanced at the clock on the wall, her heard thudding. There wasn't much time. "I brought something for you to see," she told her grandparents, turning to find her suitcase, which Rudy had leaned against the wall behind her.

"Presents aren't till Christmas Day," Grandpa scolded her. "You know that."

Charlotte laughed as she removed a thick folder from the inside of her suitcase. "This isn't anything yet. Just some drawings."

"That's right! Your mother said you were taking some art classes," Grandma Dee said. "You were always so talented, Char."

Charlotte beamed as she opened the folder on the dining room table and began to filter through the illustrations she'd made, all of which she'd painted with a mix of watercolors, oil pastels, and oil paints. The paintings displayed the mountains in upstate New York, a beautiful princess, a handsome hero, and finally, a castle that resembled the Cherry Inn. When she glanced up, she found her Grandpa and Grandma spellbound, gazing down at the illustrations with disbelief.

"It's our story, Dee," Grandpa breathed. "Look at that."

"They're just examples of how I visualize the book," Charlotte went on hurriedly. "Obviously, I have a lot of work to do. But I'm already talking to a publisher about writing and illustrating my own book. We're thinking of calling it *A Fairy Tale Christmas*."

Grandpa Hank's eyes glistened with tears. He draped his arm over Grandma's shoulders and blinked at Charlotte with disbelief.

"Of course, you'll be credited as co-writers," Charlotte went on. "I've added many embellishments to the story, so there will still be surprises when you read it."

"We're not co-writers," Grandma Dee scolded her.

"That's the silliest thing I ever heard," Charlotte said. "You and Grandpa told the story of how you settled into the Cherry Inn every year."

"Every year!" Rudy agreed, taking another Christmas cookie.

"That was just a silly story your grandfather made up," Grandma Dee said, her cheeks blotchy as she smiled.

"It wasn't silly," Rudy and Charlotte shot back in unison.

"We loved it," Rudy assured them. "And Charlotte's pushing that story into the world. More people need to know about it."

Grandma and Grandpa took a long moment to go through all of the illustrations and to compliment the delicacy of the pine trees, the heaps of snow, and the gorgeous fine lines of the "castle" of the Cherry Inn. Even the hero and princess of the story resembled Grandma and Grandpa back when they'd first purchased the Cherry Inn— a time Charlotte had romanticized over the years. She'd never imagined she'd find her handsome hero, too.

"When is this book coming out?" Grandpa Hank whispered.

"Everything moves so slowly in the publishing world," Charlotte admitted. "If not next Christmas, then the one after that. It depends on how much time I have to illustrate this year."

She wouldn't have as much time as she'd planned for, she knew. But Charlotte couldn't complain about that. She shivered with optimism.

There was a knock at the door. Louise looked flustered. "I thought everyone was already here!" She walked across the living room, and Charlotte followed behind her, leaving her illustrations spread across the table.

At the door was the handsomest man in all of Manhattan— Peter O'Shean. With his dark hair and dark eyes, his black pea coat, his slick suit jacket, and his black pointy shoes, he looked as though he'd stepped out of the pages of *GQ Magazine*. One thing he'd told her early on in his relationship with Charlotte was, *"If you don't take yourself seriously, how are you going to expect everyone else to?"* This was part of the reason Charlotte had pushed herself to start illustrating.

Louise peered at Peter with distrust in her eyes. It was a classic story of a small-town woman versus a big-city guy. "Who are you?"

"Mom, this is Peter," Charlotte interrupted. "He's my fiancé."

Peter raised his lips into a smile. Charlotte tried to detect any sense of fear or lack of confidence in his face, but there was nothing. "Pleasure to meet you, Ms. Summers," he said, extending his hand to shake. "This is a beautiful inn. Charlotte has told me so much about it."

Louise's cheeks were pink. Nobody was immune to Peter O'Shean's charms.

"Please," she said. "Come in."

Peter stepped into the foyer of the inn, where Charlotte wrapped her arms around him and burrowed her face in his chest. He smelled like the crisp snow and wintry air. Only a whiff of the city and its gas fumes and garbage remained. Not for the first time, Charlotte imagined convincing Peter to move out to White Plains after they got married. Although he dressed like a businessman, he was more-or-less between jobs at the moment. Perhaps he could help Grandma and Grandpa out at the inn for a while. Perhaps he could use that shatteringly special intellect and boost the inn's revenue into the stratosphere.

If Charlotte was honest with herself, she'd run off to the city for reasons that were no longer clear to her. She'd longed for a big, wild, impossible life. But before she'd met Peter, she'd felt aimless and very lonely. She'd eaten a diet of bad pasta and street pizza, and she'd felt her dreams slipping through her fingers.

"Who is this, then?" Grandpa Hank smiled at Peter as he strode through the living room.

"Apparently, this is Charlotte's fiancé," Louise said, crossing her arms over her chest. She watched Peter's every move as though she suspected he was about to take a log from the fireplace and set the rest of the inn ablaze.

"Goodness!" Grandpa Hank enveloped Peter in a hug as Grandma Dee jumped up and down, showing more energy than most women her age. "Isn't that something to celebrate?"

After that, there was chaos for a few minutes. Cousins, aunts, uncles, and grandparents rushed around the room, hugging Charlotte and Peter and congratulating them on this "enormous and beautiful step." Charlotte heard Peter's voice over everyone else's, thanking them with that firm and stoic tone she loved so much. That voice had nourished her in the lonely city; it had been something to hang onto in the storm.

As the congratulations died down, Grandpa Hank placed his hands on his hips and heaved a very happy sigh. Across the table, Charlotte wrapped her arm around Peter's waist and matched her grandfather's grin. She felt, in bringing Peter home as a surprise, she'd accomplished something. She'd proven herself worthy.

"Your fiancé was just showing us her gorgeous illustrations," Grandpa Hank said, gesturing toward the paintings between them on the table. "She's so talented, isn't she?"

"She is," Peter said. "I've watched her spend many nights working. Sometimes, she abandons her schoolwork and just paints and paints." He laughed.

"It's true," Charlotte said. "And then, I have to scramble to catch back up."

"It won't matter next year," Grandpa Hank went on. "After this book comes out, you'll be a world-famous children's writer. You can quit school and travel the world."

"Don't tell her to quit school," Grandma Dee teased. "Education is important."

Charlotte laughed. "I haven't decided what I'll do if the book gets successful. I'm just going to enjoy the ride."

"Good plan," Grandma Dee said.

"That's right," Peter continued. "It's just a children's book, you know?"

Peter's comment hung heavy in the air for a moment.

"What do you mean?" Rudy asked finally, his smile still plastered on his face.

"I mean," Peter continued, "if it was a big literary accomplishment, maybe Charlotte would consider dropping out of school. But it's just a bunch of paintings for kids, you know? It's probably better to set her sights higher. Right, Charlotte?"

Charlotte felt as though she'd been smacked. Similar to Rudy, she kept her smile firm. "That's probably right," she said. "Just a children's book. It's not going to break any intellectual records. It definitely won't win a Nobel Prize!" Charlotte laughed extra-hard, wanting to let her family know she was in on the joke. That she agreed with Peter.

"Well," Grandma Dee said, then cleared her throat. "Why don't we sit down in the dining room? I have some snacks prepared."

Quietly, Rudy, Bethany, a few aunts and uncles turned on their heels and headed for the dining room. Charlotte laced her fingers through Peter's and smiled up at him. "Isn't this place just magical?"

"Charlotte?" Louise interjected. "Could you help me in the kitchen for a second?"

Charlotte locked eyes with her mother. Her mother's expression was hard as stone. "I'll be right back," she told Peter. "Wait for me in the dining room, okay?"

Charlotte followed her mother into her grandparents' apartment, which was attached to the inn. Her mother and her mother's siblings had been raised in the apartment, which had allowed Grandpa and Grandma to breeze in and out of their home and work life as they pleased. There had been no such thing as work-life balance.

In the kitchen of the apartment, Louise pulled an apple pie from the oven.

"What can I help you with?" Charlotte's voice was higher pitched than she'd planned for.

Louise turned and removed oven mitts from her hands. "So that's your fiancé?"

Charlotte swallowed. "I wanted to surprise you."

"I'm surprised, all right," Louise said. "And he's certainly handsome."

Charlotte furrowed her brow.

"But I have to say, Charlotte," Louise went on, "I think you're making a mistake."

Charlotte let out a soft laugh. "You don't even know him."

"He's been here three minutes, and he's already insulted you," Louise shot. "That isn't the kind of man I want my daughter to marry. I don't even want him to stay another second in the Cherry Inn. Look at that hair, Charlotte! He looks like an evil villain in a comic book!"

Charlotte's eyes filled with tears so that her mother's face blurred. She hated that her chin quivered with rage and sorrow. "He's just nervous," Charlotte stated. "He didn't mean what he said."

"That's the kind of man who will always take you down a peg," Louise went on. "He will always see your weakness and point to it in front of everyone."

"He's not like that," Charlotte blared, crossing her arms over her chest. It was rare that she and her mother had an argument like this. The last time had been maybe eight years ago— something to do with a tank top Louise had deemed inappropriate to wear to school.

"Honey." Louise rubbed her temples and stared at the ground. She suddenly looked much older than her forty-one years. "I don't want you to end up like me."

Charlotte flared her nostrils. "Peter isn't like dad."

"He's just like him," Louise blurted. "Mark my words. He'll be out the door the minute things get hard."

"Why are you doing this? Why are you making this so hard?" Charlotte demanded. "I wanted to bring my fiancé home to meet my family! I wanted us to have a cozy Christmas together!" Charlotte's thoughts raced. "Can you please just give him another chance?"

Louise wrapped her hair into a tight ponytail. "Honey. I know you don't have much experience with men. Listen to me. Listen to reason."

"Mom," Charlotte blared. "I'm pregnant, okay? You're too late."

At this, Louise's jaw dropped. The news hung between them, separating them on either side of the kitchen. She hadn't wanted to tell her mother like this. She'd imagined a gorgeous evening by the fire and her mother weeping with joy and telling Charlotte that being a mother had been the greatest gift of her life. She hadn't pictured her mother's blotchy face or her rage.

"Oh, honey." Louise dropped her head and shook it. She was on the brink of tears, but they weren't happy ones.

"Mom, it's going to be good," Charlotte said, her voice breaking. "Peter and I love each other. We're so happy about the baby."

Louise turned and pressed her hands over her face as though just looking at Charlotte was too painful.

"Mom." Charlotte cleared the distance between them and touched her mother's shoulder. She needed her mother to get on board with this; she needed her mother's love.

But the moment Louise felt Charlotte's hand upon her shoulder, she bristled and gave her a sideways look of anger. "Don't come crying to me when he shows you who he really is," she said. "Don't say I didn't warn you."

Charlotte drew her hand back immediately and let it drop to her side. She felt as though her mother had just punched her in the stomach. She couldn't breathe. Her mother returned her attention to the counter, which she'd begun to scrub with a sponge, her elbow swinging forth and back. Charlotte swam through potential things to say. But there was nothing to take away the sting of her mother's words.

Charlotte walked like a ghost back through the apartment door and into the inn. At the dining room table, she found Peter eating a cookie and telling Rudy about New York City, about how alive it felt on the streets, even late at night. Rudy's eyes were dull with boredom.

"Hey, Peter?" Charlotte interrupted him.

Peter stopped mid-sentence and looked her way.

"Could I speak to you for a moment?" Charlotte asked.

Peter nodded toward Rudy. "Excuse me for a second."

Charlotte dragged Peter back to the foyer of the inn. Her legs quivered beneath her, threatening to cast her to the ground. "We have to go," she said, her breathing ragged. "We have to go back to the city right now."

"What happened?" Peter asked. His cheeks fell.

"I'll explain in the car," Charlotte hissed. While Charlotte had taken the bus, Peter had driven. This made for an easy escape with Peter's car.

Peter raised his shoulders. "Fine by me. I'll get your suitcase," he said. "Let's get on the road."

With the rest of her family in the dining room, laughing and gossiping over pie, Charlotte bundled up her illustrations and slipped the folder back into her suitcase. With a final glance at the illuminated Christmas tree and the crackling fire, she bolted through the foyer and out onto the front porch. By the time she'd buckled herself into the passenger seat of Peter's car, she'd worked herself into a frenzy. Tears drifted down her cheeks. Peter hit the gas pedal too hard, and she flung forward.

"Let's get out of this two-bit town, huh?" Peter said, touching her thigh as he whizzed along Main Street, ten miles over the speed limit. "Let's go back to the city where we belong."

Chapter Six

Present Day

Two days after Charlie met Charlotte Summers at Rudy's bar, he found himself on the sidewalk in front of the Cherry Inn. As usual, he'd left his car back at the cabin, and he felt refreshed and sporty after yet another stroll through the snowy woods. On the way, he'd watched three chipmunks playing along the branches of an old oak, scurrying in and out of little holes. He'd felt like a little kid, captivated by nature.

To Charlie, the Cherry Inn was a perfect blend of three elements: historical architecture, small-town charm, and ornate features that made the old structure like something out of a fairy tale book. He could already picture it on the front cover of *Architecture Digest*, along with an article called something like: "Why You Should Spend Christmas in a Family-Run Inn." With his help, he knew this place could be back up and running by next Christmas, with guests milling in and out, sitting on the porch swing with mulled wine or waving from the windows, their cheeks ruddy as they settled into the warm interior.

"Hey there." Charlotte's voice rang out from the front porch. She stood in the crack of the doorframe, smiling in a way that made it clear she wasn't sure about him.

Charlie stepped onto the porch and strode toward her, eyeing the busted porch swing on the floor and the cracked windows.

"Time has really had its way with this old place," Charlotte said with a sigh as she cranked the door open wider.

"This is nothing," Charlie assured her. "Easy fixes."

Charlotte laughed, and the sound was heavenly. "I don't know whether to believe you or not."

Charlie followed Charlotte into the foyer, where he stood along a dusty mahogany front desk, gazing at the beautiful wooden cubby holes that, once upon a time, had held iron keys for the suites upstairs. Charlotte closed the door behind them and crossed her arms. It seemed she was always closing herself off.

"Have you 'flipped' old inns like this before?" Charlotte asked, breaking through the strained silence.

"A few," Charlie said. "I fell in love with Bar Harbor about ten years ago, and I spent a summer there, buying and flipping inns."

What he didn't tell her, of course, was that they'd only gone to Bar Harbor because Sarah's family was from there, that one of the inns had belonged to Sarah's cousin.

"Do you have photographs of your work?"

"I can send you my website. You can find anything about my work there. Photographs, articles, and testimonials from previous clients. Do you know who Baxter Bailey is? I've worked with him for many years. He backs my projects." Charlie was babbling. He took a small step forward, and Charlotte inched back. Charlie wasn't accustomed to this. Back in the city, women were continually drawn to him; they made excuses to whisper in his ear or touch his back. Sarah had always told him he was too handsome for his own good, that he drove people crazy. When she'd said this, he'd always shaken his head, refusing a statement he more-or-less understood to be true. But his charms were nothing to Charlotte. She looked at him the same way you'd look at a sign above a storefront or a normal-looking tree. He didn't want this to bother him, but it did.

After a brief pause, Charlotte cleared her throat and said, "I haven't heard of Baxter Bailey, no." She turned on her heel and beckoned for him to follow her through the foyer and into the main living room, where furnishings had been covered with white sheets, the fireplace was filled with ash, paintings were crooked on the walls, and the hardwood was in dire need of polishing.

"It looks slightly haunted in here," Charlie tried to joke.

Charlotte raised her shoulders but remained quiet. Charlie watched her eyes, noting how they seemed to scan everything. They were heavy with nostalgia, as though, upon every square inch of the old place, she felt the ache of long-ago memories.

"Like I said at the bar," Charlotte began, "I don't mind selling it next year. I just want my grandfather to be comfortable."

"Why don't you let me take a crack at it?" Charlie spoke too quickly, nearly scrambling his words. "It's a gorgeous space. There's so much potential here."

Charlotte locked eyes with Charlie's. Charlie's diaphragm spasmed.

"I can't tell if you're just a sweet-talking Manhattan-ite," Charlotte said, raising her eyebrow. "Maybe you're just saying pretty things to get what you want."

Charlie laughed nervously. It wasn't every day you met a woman who spoke her mind like this, to the point of rudeness.

"But I can't figure out why you would lie," Charlotte continued. "You'll probably lose money on this project. So, let me ask you. What's in it for you?"

"I just want to make something beautiful," Charlie stuttered. "Something that has nothing to do with a high-rise building for very rich people. Something that has a link to history."

Charlotte tilted her head. The stoic expression she'd worn since he'd arrived softened. He felt as though he was on trial in her mind, as though she weighed up the pros and cons of knowing him and letting him work at the inn, taking stock of his hairstyle and his clothing and his clear privilege in the world. There was so much she couldn't know about him, even as she dug into him like this.

Finally, Charlotte threw up her hands. "What's the process of something like this?"

Charlie's heartbeat quickened. *Finally*, he thought. He had something to do with his hands, something that had nothing to do with the dark memories in the back of his mind.

"I'll draw up some plans," Charlie said. "And I'll show them to you in a few days. How does that sound?"

Charlotte's cheek twitched as though something had just occurred to her, as though she wanted to call it all off.

But somewhere behind the living room wall came the sound of a wailing baby. It was hard to imagine anywhere near that sparse living room being hospitable for humans. Charlie remembered there was an apartment attached to the inn, that this was where Charlotte's grandfather lived full-time.

"I have to run," Charlotte admitted. "My daughter just had a baby, and I'm helping out as much as I can. I hate to admit it, but I forgot how hard it is when they're so little. When they need so much."

Charlie's heart thudded with memories of his own. Instead of agreeing with her or showing her an ounce of his own honesty, he said, "Thanks for this opportunity, by the way. Can I walk around a little bit more and get the lay of the land?"

"Of course. There's a key beneath the mat out front. Lock out when you go."

Charlotte disappeared through the back door of the living room, where it looked like she entered an intermediate room that led to the front door of the family apartment. Charlie inspected this after she'd arrived safely on the other side. Already, the baby had been quieted, and Charlie could hear the soft murmurs of Charlotte and another woman, her daughter, through the door. A part of him wanted to stand there and feel the vibrations of their sentences through the wood, to feel a part of the dynamics of their loving family. It had been ages since he'd felt he belonged to something real.

When he finally managed to pull himself away from the apartment door, Charlie walked around the Cherry Inn for over an hour, envisioning its future. He crept up the staircase, which was surprisingly stable, entered each of the suites, and even turned on his phone for the first time to make notes to himself. Already, he'd begun to anticipate guests from the elite Manhattan crowd, who required a different sort of luxury than the typical small-town inns often offered. One of the inns he'd flipped in Bar Harbor had gone on to be deemed a five-star hotel, with guests paying upwards of fifteen-hundred dollars a night to stay in its suites. If he focused, he could push the Cherry Inn in that direction. He imagined the article written about his quest: **"Charlie Bryant has done it again."** The minute the idea came into his mind, he shook it away again. He thought he didn't care about the accolades. Maybe he wasn't as immune to praise as he thought.

But with his phone back on, text messages began to pepper in— at first slowly and then all at once, with messages from email, Skype, and different texting services dinging in wildly. Many of them were from Timothy, alternating between demanding to know where he was and thanking him for the sizeable Christmas bonus Charlie had sent. Many were from Baxter Bailey and Baxter's secretary, inquiring about his "new project" outside of the city. And several more messages were from women he'd recently gone on dates with, none of whom he wanted to see again. To them, he seemed lonely, dark, and brooding, which was exactly the sort of man many women wanted to "change" and to "save." He knew he was beyond saving. Probably Charlotte could sense that, too. That's why she looked at him that way. Before they could pester him more, Charlie turned his phone to Airplane mode, bent on never returning to the real world again. He had a job to do.

* * *

All night, the following day, and the morning after that, Charlie labored over his plans for the Cherry Inn. In his little cabin in the woods, he spent the hours at the table by the fire, his glasses drawn over the bridge of his nose, sketching with his pencil as the fire crackled and spat. Frequently, he paused to draw a knife over the tip of his pencil, sharpening it in the way he remembered his own grandfather sharpening his pencils so many years ago. In the evenings, Charlie alternated between stiff whiskey, some good stuff he picked up at the White Plains liquor store, and black coffee, and he fell through dreamlands, imagining the Cherry Inn not only coming back to life— but having a brand-new spirit. People would journey from miles around to enter the gorgeous, fairy tale-like Victorian home. But beyond the historical exterior, they would enter into a state-of-the-art interior with glass walls, a modern and sleek fireplace, and contemporary art paintings. The suites upstairs would be modern, the bathroom walls made of stone, and the showers like waterfalls. Gone would be this "cutesy" inn feel. That was one of the reasons people had stopped coming to the Cherry Inn in the first place, he decided. People didn't want cutesy anymore. They liked history— but they wanted to take a photograph of the exterior of the historical inn and then enjoy the luxurious interior, which transported the inn to the twenty-first century.

This was how he would save the inn.

After nearly forty-eight hours of sketching, pondering, erasing, and designing, Charlie decided he needed to leave the cabin again. The night before, there'd been nearly six inches of snow, and in the fresh light of the morning, he trudged through in his snow boots, adjusting his leather bag filled with his designs over his shoulder.

He remembered seeing an adorable diner just off of Main Street in White Plains, and he had a hunch they had everything he currently craved, including bacon, eggs, and blueberry pancakes. Perhaps his diet of sandwiches, soups, and whiskey wasn't cutting it anymore.

The diner was called Jeez, Louise, and it was little more than a hut with ten booths. There was a jukebox in the corner, and mirrors hung on most of the walls. A woman in her late sixties carried a pot of coffee as she whisked through the tables, her legs muscular from a life-time of waitressing. She greeted Charlie with an easy smile and said, "Take any booth."

Charlie slid into a booth near the window. Without asking, the woman placed a cup on his table and filled it with black coffee. "How are you doing this fine day, sir?"

"Just fine," Charlie said. "Hungry."

"You're in the right place," the woman said.

Charlie ordered exactly what he'd come for— eggs over-easy, bacon crispy, and blueberry pancakes, the extra tall stack. The woman didn't write anything down. Proba-bly, waitresses like her had better memories than most people in the world; probably, they could have handled world politics better than most leaders due to their cool-ness in the face of stress.

As Charlie waited for his food, he pulled out his designs for the Cherry Inn and splayed them across the table. In the back was the sound of spitting grease. The smell of batter on the griddle filled the air. Maybe he would gain a few pounds out here. Maybe he'd finally lose that "Manhattan six-pack" he'd worked so hard for. He imagined what Timothy would say if he saw him: "Char-lie, I've signed you up for a meeting with your personal trainer. It's time." But Charlie never wanted to see a personal trainer again. He wanted to eat pancakes. He wanted to laugh more. He wanted to inhale the goodness of this small town.

When the waitress arrived with an enormous breakfast platter, she stopped before she put the plate down and inspected the designs across the table. Charlie beamed with pride.

"What's all this?" she asked.

"Do you know the Cherry Inn?"

The woman arched her eyebrow. "I've heard of it."

"Yes. I figured, in such a small town, you would have. Well, I'm a developer, and I'm going to flip it! Look." Charlie traced his finger through the design of the new, modern, and sleek foyer, explaining his concept. "People don't want 'cute inns' anymore. They want to feel a part of history without actually dropping themselves into history. You know?"

"I think I do," the woman said, still holding up his breakfast platter.

"And here, look," Charlie went on, gesturing toward his plans for one of the upstairs rooms. "This has been the library, which obviously doesn't bring in any revenue for the inn. My plan is to tear down this wall and make this the biggest suite in the entire inn. With the right accoutrements, the owners can charge an arm and a leg for people to stay in this suite. Especially because the window of the library overlooks Main Street."

The woman's cheek twitched. She hadn't smiled once throughout Charlie's entire presentation.

"And here..." Charlie pointed toward the living room. "I was thinking..."

"Let me get this straight," the woman interrupted.

"The owners have hired you to design a modern Cherry Inn?"

Charlie stuttered. "Yes?"

The woman's eyes became slits. Charlie had never struggled to read someone's expression more. He couldn't tell if she was impressed or just bored. And then, all at once, she slammed his breakfast platter down in the center of his designs, casting grease and syrup across a few of the drawings. "Hey!" Charlie cried.

But the woman had already fled. She smashed her hands against the door to open it and marched out into the chill, abandoning the diner and all its current guests without a second thought. Charlie gaped at her as she walked away, disappearing around the corner. "What the heck?" he muttered, removing the breakfast platter from his drawings and setting them off to the side to dry. The designs were still clear; he could simply transfer the drawings to clean sheets. Not all was lost. But still, he had the strangest sensation that he'd just been reprimanded by his mother in public. He couldn't shake it.

Chapter Seven

Charlotte sat in her grandfather's La-Z-Boy, watching *The Big Bang Theory* on low volume. In her arms, Ethan slept, his mouth open, his chin raised, and his tiny hand splayed across her upper chest as though he wanted to feel the beating of her heart. In their bedrooms, Grandpa Hank and Van both slept as well, Van ailing due to a terrible case of mastitis that had come on very suddenly. This was yet another thing Charlotte had forgotten about so many years after her own babies had been born. She'd forgotten that being a new mother meant being an exposed nerve, your body being used to its breaking point.

But little Ethan was perfect. He was two weeks old, safe, and warm in his great-grandparents' apartment, miles and miles away from his evil father. As Charlotte held him, she dared herself to think back to twenty-eight years ago, after she'd given birth to Van. She'd still been very in love with Peter. Even when Peter hadn't helped her with Van or when he'd gone out with his friends when she, herself, had had mastitis, Charlotte had worshipped him. How could she have been so blind? She'd always known herself to be an intelligent person— the best in her English class, the one friends called in a pinch for advice. How was it possible she'd fallen for the worst-possible man? And now, Van had done the same.

Charlotte had wanted something different for Van. Just as her mother had wanted something different for Charlotte. Life was a constant cycle of repetitions. It seemed impossible to ever break your patterns.

Suddenly, the front door burst open. The movement was so swift that Charlotte jumped to her feet, waking little Ethan, who gurgled and then wailed, his red fist pumping. But Ethan's fear was the least of Charlotte's worries. Standing on the welcome mat in her waitressing uniform was Louise Summers. She glowered at Charlotte, her eyes penetrating. It was the first time they'd seen one another in years, and it alarmed Charlotte to see how much her mother had aged. Probably, her mother was thinking the same thing about her.

Finally, Charlotte managed to speak. "Where is your coat? It's fifteen degrees out there!"

Louise crossed her arms over her chest. If she was cold, she wouldn't confess to it. "I can't believe you'd do this."

In her arms, Ethan had quieted, seemingly too curious about the woman in the doorway to make a fuss, and she adjusted him gently to ensure he was more comfortable. Blowing all the air from her lungs, she crossed the living room and closed the door again, praying that all this racket hadn't woken Van up. She needed her rest.

"Can you update me on why you're angry with me today?" Charlotte said. "I can't always keep up."

"I really thought you loved this place, Charlotte,"

Louise said. "I know we've had our differences over the years, but I thought, in your heart of hearts, you'd always respect the Cherry Inn."

"I do! I always have!" Charlotte sputtered. She wanted to point out that the Summers family hadn't lent the inn half the respect it deserved— that they'd let it fall into disrepair.

"I should have known," Louise said. "All that money and fame went to your head."

Charlotte couldn't help but laugh at the statement. "What money? What fame? What on earth are you talking about, Mom?" Because Charlotte had published one semi-successful children's book and six not-so-successful children's books, her mother had built up an idea of Charlotte's life that just didn't exist.

Louise's eyes were fiery. "You want to destroy the spirit of this place. You want to cleanse it of any history. And I won't let you do it."

"Can you please clue me in on what you're talking about?" Charlotte demanded. "I'm lost here."

"You always make it about yourself," Louise said.

Ethan took this opportunity to open his mouth and wail again. Immediately, Louise bristled and blinked down at the tiny baby in Charlotte's arms, although she was noticing him for the first time. Because she'd ignored all of Charlotte and Van's messages since their arrival, she hadn't yet come over to meet her great-grandson. Now, her face softened, and she took a delicate step forward. Her eyes glinted with tears.

It was always like this with Louise: emotions running amok from one end of the emotional spectrum to the other. It always gave Charlotte whiplash.

"That's him, then?" Louise cupped her hands

together. "He's just so tiny. Look at that little hand."

Charlotte could barely hear her mother over Ethan's wails. It seemed impossible that such a little thing could emit such tremendous noise. Already, a headache crawled up the back of Charlotte's neck and planted itself between her ears. Van's door burst open, and she hurried out, her face pale from pain. When she saw Louise, she stalled and said, "Oh! Grandma. Hi? Um. Good to see you?"

Louise melted even more at the sight of her granddaughter, a young woman she'd hardly ever gotten to know. Charlotte wanted to remind Louise that this was her own fault, that she'd drawn a boundary between them. Van extended her arms to take Ethan from Charlotte, then carried him to the attached kitchen, where she procured a bottle from the fridge and proceeded to feed him. Throughout, Louise and Charlotte watched her. Charlotte's heart throbbed with memories of having to do this for Van— of being so needed on a physical level. Was Louise thinking the same thing about Charlotte?

The crying stopped, and the silence was heavy. The only sound was of Ethan sucking on the bottle; his soft eyelids had begun to close.

"Sorry about that," Van whispered. "We're still trying to find a rhythm around here."

Louise looked deflated, like a warrior who'd just traveled to battle to find her opponents ailing and unable to fight. She leaned against the doorway and crossed her arms tighter.

"You'll find it," Louise whispered, reaching up to swipe a tear away from her cheek.

It had been a long time since Charlotte had seen her mother cry. Even that night of their first big fight, when

Charlotte had told Louise about her pregnancy, Louise's face had been a giant, cherry-red tomato, filled with rage. There had been no tears on her part. Charlotte had assumed she'd been the only one to mourn their lost mother-daughter relationship. She'd assumed her mother had moved on stoically; such was the way of Louise Summers.

"I'd better go." Louise spun on her heel and turned the doorknob, whipping herself back into the frigid air.

Charlotte leaped toward the window to watch her mother trace the path around the back of the inn, headed toward Main Street and back to Jeez, Louise, the diner she'd opened and run mostly by herself since the age of twenty-five. Her face looked frantic, and she walked gingerly as though she'd recently hurt her foot.

"What was that about?" Van asked.

Charlotte clucked her tongue. "I wish I understood."

Van leaned against the counter. "Did she say something about your money and fame?"

"She did. Have you seen my money and fame anywhere? I seem to have lost them."

Van's laughter was sorrowful. In her arms, Ethan had fallen back to sleep, and she placed the bottle back on the counter and adjusted him in her arms. "Why does Grandma treat you like that??"

Charlotte couldn't catch her breath.

"I mean, she treats you like you did something really horrible to her," Van went on. "And I've never been able to figure that out."

It was true that Charlotte had never explained to Van the dynamics of her and Louise's relationship. But to drudge up the past in explanation meant translating how much Van's birth had affected the way Louise had treated

74

her— which was cruel. It was better for Van to think that Charlotte and Louise had never seen eye to eye.

"She never liked me," Charlotte offered with a shrug. "I've spent my life wondering why."

Grandpa Hank's bedroom door creaked open, and Grandpa Hank wandered out of his bedroom sleepily, rubbing his eyes. He wore a pair of soft blue pajamas, and his gray hair was like a cirrus cloud. Charlotte felt a surge of love for him.

"Did you have a good nap?" she asked, hurrying to get him a glass of water and his pills, which he usually took after his late-morning nap.

"I did," Grandpa Hank said. "Until I thought I heard my youngest daughter out here, yapping away. Was it a nightmare?"

"It wasn't," Charlotte said, pressing the water glass into his hands. "Mom just wanted to stop in and say hi."

Grandpa Hank shook his head sadly. "My Louise has always been a drama queen. I adore her to pieces, but I'll never understand her. Perhaps understanding our children is too much to ask for."

"I definitely don't always understand this little guy," Van joked, nodding toward Ethan. "If only he could tell me what was wrong!"

"Language has nothing to do with it," Grandpa Hank said.

Charlotte sighed. "Mom was accusing me of all sorts of stuff. She said I didn't respect the inn. And that all my money and fame had changed me?"

Grandpa Hank chuckled gently and placed a medicine tablet on his tongue. "Why didn't you bring any of that money to White Plains with you?"

"I would have if I had it, Grandpa," Charlotte assured

him. She didn't want to get into it too much: the endless parade of bills she still needed to pay, which awaited her on her desk in Manhattan; the ever-rising prices of everything in the city, from groceries to utilities to meals out at restaurants. Manhattan had been her world since she'd turned eighteen, a time of exhilaration and hope. But the city had slowly been rejecting her for many years at this point. She was like a splinter in Manhattan's big toe, being pushed out.

Grandpa Hank was quiet for a moment, his eyes gray and distant. Outside, snow fluttered and blew in circles; the wind rushed against the house, and the walls creaked.

"Louise has been alone for a long time," Grandpa Hank said finally. "She's got a lot of different ideas about the world, and it's difficult to convince her otherwise."

"Stubbornness runs in the Summers' women," Van offered kindly. "I think it's served me well over the years."

Grandpa Hank smiled. "Louise has always taken that stubbornness a bridge too far. Your mother knows that better than anyone." He nodded toward Charlotte and took another swig of water. "But I've never been able to reason with her. I have never been able to tell her just how big a mistake it was to push you away. I imagine she knows somewhere in that broken heart of hers. The question is, will she ever let herself forgive you and herself and move on?"

Van peered at Charlotte curiously, sensing the tremendous story beneath Grandpa Hank's words.

"It looks like she's just finding new reasons to get angry at me," Charlotte whispered with a playful shrug.

"Never a dull day in White Plains," Grandpa Hank said finally, trudging back toward his La-Z-Boy and dropping himself onto the cushion. "You ladies thought you'd get some peace and quiet away from the city. Buckle up! Who knows what will happen next?"

With Grandpa Hank distracted with the television, rocking gently in his chair, Van waved to get Charlotte's attention and beckoned for her to follow her into her bedroom. Long ago, this bedroom had been Charlotte's Aunt Tina's, Louise's older sister, and there were still relics of that time: Aunt Tina's posters of Elvis and the Beatles and her old-fashioned sewing machine, with which she'd sewed both her and Louise's prom dresses. They'd set up a diaper changing area for Ethan near the window, and they'd purchased a crib from the superstore near the highway, where Van now placed Ethan.

"What is Great-Grandpa talking about?" Van rasped.

Charlotte sat at the edge of Van's unmade bed. "You already know Grandma and I don't get along." She hoped that would be the end of it, that Van would take that information and be done with it.

Instead, Van pushed it. "But you never really told me or Collin why. We always wondered, you know? Like, every summer we came out to White Plains, Grandma kept her distance. It was always so weird."

"It must have felt terrible for you," Charlotte whispered. "Grandchildren should feel loved and supported by their grandparents."

"Great-Grandpa and Great-Grandma gave us all the love we really needed," Van remembered. "And it was okay. We always had a brilliant time here. It was just strange, you know?" She pressed her lips together and continued to stare out the window. "Now that I have a baby, I'm just thinking of all the possible ways I'll mess up as a parent. I'm already failing in a million small ways. But I just can't imagine avoiding Ethan like the plague, the way Louise avoids you. And I want to know about what happened, if only so I can avoid making the same mistake. If we don't learn about the past, we're doomed to repeat it. Right?"

Charlotte's heart cracked at the edges. Her daughter was wise beyond her years.

"Your grandmother felt very disrespected by my life choices," Charlotte offered finally, hoping that would be enough.

"But it's not like you ever did anything that crazy," Van tried to joke. "You don't have any tattoos. You went to college. You had both Collin and I when you were married, for goodness' sake. I mean, you're basically boring."

"Gee. Thanks."

"You know what I mean." Van laughed. "I'm tired, and not everything is coming out the way I want it to."

Charlotte touched her daughter's shoulder. Sometimes, she felt as though her love for Van had tripled in size since Ethan's birth, and that love threatened to drown her.

"Why don't you get some more sleep, honey?" Charlotte suggested. "You need to heal up and rest."

Van frowned, and a little wrinkle formed between her eyebrows. She seemed to weigh up whether she wanted to push this conversation further. Maybe she wanted to fight until Charlotte admitted what had happened twenty-eight years ago. But she collapsed at the edge of the bed and rolled into a ball.

"This isn't over," she threatened in a soft voice, shaking her finger.

"I love you, sweetie," Charlotte said, giving her hand a squeeze before she left the room. "Sleep well."

Chapter Eight

C harlie returned to the snow-capped cabin that afternoon, his stomach bulging against the waistband of his jeans, heavy with the biggest and most delicious, soul-affirming breakfast he'd eaten in many years. The strange incident with the waitress still gave him pause. He had a funny instinct to take his phone off of Airplane Mode and text someone back in Manhattan about it. "Aren't small-town people crazy?" he might write. "I never know what they'll do next."

But just as soon as he thought it, Charlie was soured with the fact that he had no idea who he would send that text to. His assistant, Timothy? Had he ever seen Timothy laugh? No, he wasn't sure he had. Beyond Timothy, however, Charlie didn't have much in the way of friends. He'd sequestered himself off from "real life" over the years, only attending social functions he was required to, ones that Timothy explained advanced his career.

What had it been like to have a best friend to share things with? Charlie racked his mind, searching for memories. There had been Jason Swartz back in high school, a guy with black curly hair and thick-rimmed glasses, with whom Charlie had discussed his fascination with the female gender. Neither of them had understood girls in the slightest, and they'd approached the concept of dating as though it were a difficult exam in school. Charlie wished he could remember the last joke he and Jason had shared. Always, in relationships that had faded, there had been a "last conversation," a "last word." Yet it was probably always so menial and boring, a last gasp of something that had already died.

Of course, Charlie could remember every single thing he and Sarah had said to one another in their final conversation. That was a blessing and a cursing.

Charlie spent the afternoon re-drawing the designs for the Cherry Inn. After he finalized them, he fed the grease-speckled pages to the fire and watched them turn to ash. He filled a glass with whiskey and sat in the warm glow of the fireplace, watching the snow outside. To distract himself, he imagined Charlotte's face when he showed her the designs for the Cherry Inn. She was extraordinarily beautiful, and he imagined her eyes widening, her plump lips parting with surprise as she inspected his precise drawings. He imagined her locking her gaze with his and breathing, "I can't believe this. They're sensational. You're a real artist."

Charlie shook with laughter at himself. He'd grown accustomed to people saying things like this to him, to endless praise. Manhattanites begged him to flip their apartments and townhouses; they ached for him to inspect their stepson's dying restaurant or their grandmother's old, haunted cinema in Queens. "Use that artistic touch to bring it into the twenty-first century, Charlie," they begged. "Please."

But Charlotte didn't know what talent she'd stumbled into in Rudy's bar. She didn't know that the single-greatest mind of property development had offered to electrify the Cherry Inn and bring it back to life.

The morning after the incident at the diner, Charlie rolled up his plans for the Cherry Inn, drank a second cup of coffee, put on his snow boots, and strode into the winter wonderland outside his door. A cardinal landed on a branch above him, a flitting red dot, and it twittered as he walked past. He filled his lungs with frigid air, and his skin tightened over his cheeks. If everything panned out, perhaps he could book the cabin for another six months, build back up the Cherry Inn, and reveal it to the world by summertime. Perhaps, from this cabin in the woods, he could watch winter melt into a gorgeous spring; he could smell the blooms as they swelled beneath a warming sun.

Charlotte was expecting him. She opened the front door of the Cherry Inn as he bucked up the front steps. Her eyes were heavy with questions.

"Morning," she said. "Can I get you a cup of coffee?"

Charlie said sure. She led him into the living room of the old inn, where she'd removed a white sheet from an ornate green couch. She urged him to sit down, then disappeared through the back door to fetch two mugs of coffee from the back apartment. She set the mugs on the coffee table before them and eyed the cylinder in Charlie's hands, in which he'd placed the plans for the Cherry Inn.

"How is it going with the new baby?" Charlie asked, surprising himself. He wasn't accustomed to wanting to make small talk.

"Oh, you know. We're just overwhelmed with love for him."

81

Charlie smiled. "Is this your first grandchild?"

"I have two granddaughters," Charlotte explained, "but they live in California."

"Oh. I'm sorry to hear that. That's a long flight."

Charlotte winced. "I try to do it once or twice a year. The girls are pretty young and don't travel well. But every time I see them, they're completely different. Because I'm not around so often, they obviously barely remember me. It breaks my heart. And gosh, it's so different to how I was raised. I was constantly here at the Cherry Inn with my grandparents. My Grandma Dee was my hero. And my Grandpa Hank is still the only real voice of reason in my life. The man is eighty-eight, and he still teaches me a little bit more every day."

Charlie had a strange instinct to touch her hand. What had gotten into him? Charlotte tugged her curls behind her ears and looked Charlie in the eye.

"Sorry. I'm blabbering." Charlotte laughed at herself and rolled her eyes. "You came here to show me what you've been working on."

"There's no rush," Charlie assured her as he reached for his designs.

"I have to confess. I went to your website. You've worked on some extraordinary projects," Charlotte went on. "That orchestra rehearsal space for the Philharmonic? I stared at those photographs for so long." Her face was rapt with attention; this was the same expression Charlie was accustomed to back in Manhattan. People so often gushed about his accomplishments, about his talents. He found it especially gorgeous on Charlotte's face. He could have listened to her compliment him all day.

"That was a fun project," Charlie admitted as he unfurled the designs out onto the coffee table. "Normally, people want to talk about the luxury hotels and apartment buildings."

"They're gorgeous, too, of course," Charlotte said.

The first design Charlie showed Charlotte was of the foyer, with its fresh glass desk and its asymmetrical chandelier. "Imagine it," he began. "People walk through the front door of this old, historical inn and find themselves in the twenty-first century. They're greeted with a glass of champagne and led to their room..." He paused to flip to another design, which showed the upstairs suite. "Here, they find themselves in the lap of luxury. Out their window, they see a beautiful view of Main Street in small-town America. Their shower is straight from a spa, and there's an in-suite jacuzzi made with stones."

Charlotte furrowed her brow with concentration.

"I have a very exciting plan for the living area," Charlie went on, bringing that design forward. "Of course, we'll get rid of all this old furniture, rip down that wall over there, and completely revamp the fireplace situation. I'm imagining a skylight over there." He pointed toward the far end of the living room. "That way, when you're here by the fireplace, you can watch the snow."

Charlie continued his presentation, pressing forward, as Charlotte remained rapt but silent. Every bit of Charlie was sure she adored his plan, his projections, and his outlook on future revenue streams. He could almost imagine her leaping to her feet after he was finished, hugging him, and thanking him for his joyful commitment to the Cherry Inn. Would he invite her to go to dinner tonight? To celebrate? It had been ages since he'd actually set up a date himself. It had been Timothy who'd pushed him into the dating world, insisting it was better for business if Charlie had a romantic partner. "People don't trust you right now. You're a dark and brooding artist type. They want to be able to meet you and your wife for dinner!" Timothy had said. This had nearly shattered Charlie.

But all at once, Charlotte was on her feet. She'd jumped up so quickly that her mug of coffee fell to the ground, and a coffee stain bled out across the hardwood.

"Shoot! Shoot." Charlotte fled the living room to fetch a towel, leaving Charlie alone. The living room continued to echo everything he'd just told her; with the dramatic plans he'd just pledged to do. He waited nervously, clutching his knees, until Charlotte returned to clean up the coffee stain.

"I'm sorry about that." Charlie wasn't sure why he was apologizing. He hadn't been the one to spill the coffee.

Charlotte pressed the towel into the coffee stain and lifted her head to look at him. Her eyes were no longer illuminated, and there was something twisted about her smile. Charlie was taken aback.

"Can I ask you a question?" Charlotte said.

"Of course. You can ask me anything you want to."

Charlotte nodded toward the plans. "Did you happen to draw these at a diner called Jeez, Louise?"

Charlie's heart thudded. "I was working there yesterday. Yes. Why?"

Charlotte rolled her shoulders back. After she mopped up the rest of the coffee, she stood and wrapped the towel in a tight ball. She turned around, looking at the living room, inspecting the cracks in the walls, the busted window and the dust-filled corners. Charlie couldn't begin to guess what she was thinking, but his stomach had begun to curdle with dread.

"What do you think used to happen here?" Charlotte asked suddenly.

Charlie stuttered. "I don't know what you mean?"

"Picture Christmas morning here at the inn," Charlotte ordered. "Imagine that heaps of grandchildren have just woken up, and they're pouring down the staircase, eager for breakfast and presents. Can you see it?"

Charlie blinked several times. All he could sense in the old space were dust and shadows.

"Okay. Imagine you're a little kid," Charlotte continued. "And your grandmother has just made the most delicious mug of hot cocoa for you. And your grandfather is going to sit you down to tell you a story. It's the same story he tells every year on Christmas Eve, but you will never get bored of it. Can you feel it?"

Charlie scrunched his face. He recognized he'd done something wrong and that Charlotte wasn't going to let him off the hook easily. But he couldn't begin to imagine what it was. He felt the same way he had when he'd forgotten his and Sarah's anniversary— a time that had been particularly marvelous for his career. He'd been yanked across the United States, from one meeting to the next, which had eventually resulted in his relationship with Baxter Bailey, which had changed everything. But when he'd returned home, Sarah had given him the cold shoulder, her eyes hard. When he'd figured out what he'd forgotten, he'd crumbled, blathered apologies, and taken her out to eat at some of the most divine restaurants in Chicago for months on-end. That was before they'd moved out east. That was ages ago.

Charlie blinked himself back to this reality. Why was Charlotte so angry?

"Oh my gosh. You can't feel it, can you?" Charlotte crossed her arms over her chest and gaped at him.

Charlie stood and glared at her. "I can feel that this place is falling apart." He hated when anyone insulted his intelligence. "I can feel that the walls are cracking, that the floors are giving way in spots. I can feel that nobody has cared a lick about this place in over a decade."

Charlotte's cheeks were blotchy. "This place is home to some of my favorite Christmas memories," she said, her voice breaking. "It was the coziest place in the world. And these designs you made?" She shook her head. "The foyer looks like a futuristic airplane. The new living room looks like a doctor's office! And I can't begin to understand your removal of the library! A small-town inn like this needs a library! And didn't you even consider how long it took my grandfather to assemble all the books in that library?"

"Some of them are moldy!"

Charlotte made her hands into fists. "Most of them are fine!"

"Most of them." Charlie rubbed his temples. "Don't you understand? This inn has gone the way of hundreds of inns across the United States. It hasn't been updated to fit the luxuries required of the modern American upper-middle-class. It's stuck in a dusty, uncomfortable past."

"Let me guess," Charlotte shot back. "You hated your childhood."

Charlie rolled his eyes. "I didn't hate my childhood. I just don't feel the need to mummify my childhood. Just like modern architecture, I've moved on."

Charlotte took a dramatic step toward him so that the tip of her nose was no more than a few inches from his. "The Cherry Inn will never look like this. The fact that you even imagined it like this is an insult to everything my grandparents built."

Charlie cackled. "This is ridiculous. Do you even know who I am?"

"Do you even know where you're standing?" Charlotte shot back.

Charlie shivered with laughter and outrage. He rolled back up his designs and shoved them into the protective cylinder, his nostrils flared. "I've never met anyone more ungrateful than you, Charlotte Summers. I'm actually impressed. I can't wait to tell everyone back in Manhattan that a nobody from White Plains rejected Charlie Bryant's designs."

"I really hope you tell them," Charlotte cried. "Tell them you've completely lost your Christmas spirit! Tell them you're an outright Ebenezer Scrooge!"

Charlie tossed his head and stomped back toward the foyer. The floorboards crackled and popped beneath him, still more proof of the tremendous work the old inn required. He wouldn't be the one to do it. Perhaps it would crumble and be little more than a heap of old stones and wooden slats three Christmases from now. What would Charlotte do with her memories, then? Oh, she would regret this day.

At the door, Charlie turned to glare back through the darkness, where Charlotte remained near the ornate couch, her arms twisted over her chest. Charlie had the sudden sensation that he was eighteen years old, bickering with his high school girlfriend. As he caught Charlotte's gaze, he forgot, momentarily, what he'd been so upset about. Couldn't they just hug and makeup? Couldn't they laugh about this?

"Do you need help with the door?" Charlotte called.

Charlie's rage filled his chest again. He yanked at the doorknob as he responded, his tone sarcastic: "Merry Christmas, Charlotte Summers. Good luck on your journey into nostalgia. I'm sure it'll get you somewhere."

"Thanks so much!" Charlotte said. "Hope to see you never again!"

Charlie stormed out of the inn and slammed the door behind him. For the next fifteen minutes, he stomped along the sidewalk, glaring at whoever passed him by, his heartbeat racing. But when he reached the forest trail, he stopped short, gasped for breath, and touched the trunk of a maple to support himself. His head swam with images of Charlotte, with the memories she'd tried to translate to him from this long-ago childhood. He shook them away. Even still, his lips quivered into a smile. What had gotten into him? Why could he still hear Charlotte's voice in his mind?

Chapter Nine

December 2003

It had been Sarah's idea to go on the road trip. As she put it, it had been a difficult few years for the two of them, and they needed a break. Their list of obligations and stressors was a mile long. For years, Charlie had traipsed from one job to the next in the Chicago suburbs, and Sarah had been working at a restaurant down the road from their apartment, slinging burgers and fries to pay what she could of the bills. Nights, she studied the law, bent on finishing undergrad and then moving on to law school. They never seemed to have quite enough money— but they managed to scrape by, often by the skin of their teeth. Charlie continued to remind Sarah that his big break was just around the corner and that people would give him a chance in the world of property development soon. Sarah believed him, even when Charlie wasn't sure if he believed in himself.

Charlie was twenty-nine, and Sarah was twenty-five. They'd been married for four years, which felt like both a long time and a very short time. Charlie felt as though Sarah was the only person who'd ever actually known him; at the same time, he felt as though they were still discovering little nuances about one another. When Charlie met people in the developer business who talked about their "thirty-five-year-long marriages," he tried and failed to imagine that much time with Sarah. It was impossible to picture them old, to imagine Sarah's face with wrinkles and gray hair on Charlie's head. This was one of the problems with being young, Charlie knew. It was impossible to remember that it wouldn't last forever.

Sarah had mapped out the road trip. On the first day, they'd taken a ferry from Chicago to the west coast of Michigan, where they'd driven up to Sleeping Bear Sand Dunes. Despite the twenty-degree chill, they'd run down the biggest sand dune either of them had ever seen. They'd then needed thirty-five minutes to crawl back up it, taking frequent breaks to gaze behind them at the turquoise blue. "The lake looks like photographs of the Mediterranean," Sarah said. Charlie promised her he'd take her to the Mediterranean someday. "Don't get ahead of yourself, Bryant," Sarah joked. "Let's get this road trip finished first. Maybe in a few decades, we can talk about getting over to Europe."

That first night, they grabbed a motel room in a tiny town and watched television, sitting up in bed. They laughed at the Michigander accent and tried to imitate it, drawing out their vowels.

"You can't do it," Sarah said. "Your accent is way too Chicago. You couldn't be from anywhere else."

"And you sound too New England for anything else," Charlie joked.

Sarah was originally from Maine. She'd moved to

Chicago at age twelve and had never fully lost her accent. Charlie had met her when she was twenty, and he was twenty-four. He'd just gotten out of a long-term relationship and hadn't been looking for anything serious. Sarah had changed his mind with the briefest glance. He'd known something in the belly of his soul, something that didn't even make sense to him at the time. She was the one. But at first, when he'd asked her out, she hadn't believed they would be anything to one another. She'd said she was in love with someone else.

In the car headed toward Niagara Falls, Charlie brought this up again. "Who were you in love with?"

Sarah eyed him from the passenger seat. "What are you talking about?"

"When we first met, you told me you were in love with someone else. You wouldn't go out with me."

Sarah laughed. "You remember that?"

"It was only five years ago."

Sarah sighed. "I was in love with my neighbor."

Charlie racked his mind, trying to remember Sarah's old neighbor. "The old guy upstairs?"

"Mr. Chancer was eighty-five years old," Sarah said. "It wasn't him."

"So, who?"

"Do you have to know everything?" Sarah asked, pretending to be disgruntled.

Charlie smiled wider and reached across the car to squeeze her hand. "I was so broken up inside when you said no. I nearly gave up on you."

"You did not," Sarah shot back. "You basically stalked me until I agreed to get that coffee with you."

Charlie laughed. He remembered it now: how he'd gone to the bars she'd frequented, eaten at the restaurant she'd worked at, and gotten to know a few of her friends better. It had all been in pursuit of this life they'd built.

"In hindsight, I should have called the police," Sarah joked.

"You still can," Charlie said.

Sarah eyed him from the passenger seat, where she had the Atlas sprawled across her lap. Charlie felt an inexplicable surge of love for her. How had he gotten so lucky?

"I'll hold off for a while," Sarah said. "At least until we make it to the Atlantic Ocean."

"You're using me for my car," Charlie said. "I knew it."

At Niagara Falls, Charlie and Sarah wore enormous ponchos, wrapped their arms around one another, and watched the water surge below. The air was nothing but a cloud, so misty that they could hardly see the other people on the platform. At the nearby restaurant, the waitress said, "We don't get that many guests during December, but I think it looks that much more magical in the winter." Charlie and Sarah agreed. They ordered club sandwiches and chips and told each other stories from their childhood, even a few they'd never shared before. Charlie had the sensation that he would always be learning new things about Sarah, even fifty years from now.

They kept driving east. Sarah wanted to go to New York City for a night to see the way Manhattan was decorated for Christmas and to buy her mother a bottle of perfume.

But fifty miles outside of New York City, Sarah turned green. She clapped her hand over her mouth and then cried out, "Pull over! Charlie, please!"

Charlie yanked the car to the side of the highway,

where Sarah pressed open the passenger door and heaved. The air was cold, and Charlie's hands were already chapped with chill. He touched her back, terrified.

"Are you okay?" Charlie asked.

Sarah heaved another few times, then turned to look up at him. "Can we stop driving for the day?"

Charlie pulled off at the next exit, which read WHITE PLAINS: 8 miles.

"White Plains," Sarah sang. "It sounds beautiful, doesn't it? Like something from a fairy tale."

"I don't know about that," Charlie said with a laugh. Maybe Sarah was delusional. What had she eaten for lunch? Had it been slightly moldy, had it gone bad? He'd read that some types of food poisoning affected your perception of the world.

Charlie pulled into a motel on the outskirts of White Plains and got them a room. Sarah cozied up under the blankets of the bed and turned on the television.

"I guess I'll order pizza?" Charlie said, frowning down at his wife. She still looked very pale.

"Extra black olives," Sarah said. "And extra onions."

Charlie laughed. "Sounds great." If her appetite was intact, she couldn't be too sick.

The pizza arrived twenty-five minutes later. Charlie put the pizza on the bed between them, and they watched television for a little while. Sarah ate her pizza quickly, as though she were suddenly ravenous, and Charlie eyed her every few seconds, realizing that she hadn't said a word to him since the pizza had arrived. It was rare that he and Sarah ever shut up around each other.

Charlie wiped his hands on a napkin. He suddenly felt panicked. What if Sarah had suddenly realized something about him? What if she'd realized she was unhappy in their marriage? They knew plenty of people who'd gotten divorced in their twenties. They called it the "first wave of divorce" in a way that suggested they, themselves, would never breakup. But people never thought they were going to break up until they did. He suddenly felt terribly sick.

"Sarah," Charlie blurted. "Will you just tell me what I did wrong? I want to fix it. I'll do anything."

Sarah blinked at him, her lips shining with grease from the pizza. Her dark-blonde hair was mussed from so many days on the road, and her eye makeup was smudged. He'd never seen anyone more beautiful.

"It's just that we've hardly talked since we got to White Plains," Charlie went on. "And I'm overthinking everything."

Sarah's lips quivered with laughter. Charlie felt as though he wasn't in on her joke, and his cheeks burned with embarrassment.

"I'm sorry, Charlie," Sarah said with a laugh. "I really am."

Charlie straightened his spine. Was this it? Her big reveal about her affair with the fry cook at the restaurant? Her assertions that Charlie was never "the one for her," after all?

"I found out when we were back in Niagara," Sarah continued. "But I wanted to wait for the perfect time. I wanted to tell you at the top of the Empire State Building like I was Meg Ryan or something."

Charlie gaped at her. Despite having known her for five years, he felt he had no idea what she was talking about. It was as though she spoke another language.

Finally, Sarah rolled her eyes, and her face broke into

the most gorgeous smile he'd ever seen. "I'm pregnant, you dummy," she said. "You're going to be a father."

Charlie rocketed to his feet and stared at her. He was no longer on solid ground, no longer in White Plains or on planet Earth. The world as he'd understood it before this moment was inexplicably changed. "A father," he whispered.

And then, he fell back onto the bed and wrapped his bride in his arms, covering her with kisses. This was the future they'd always planned for. Despite their pathetic bank account, they would find a way to make it through. They would do it for the love of one another and the love they already had for the little bean inside Sarah— a future they could hang their lives upon.

Chapter Ten

Present Day

C harlotte stormed back into the apartment behind the Cherry Inn and pulled her hair into a tight ponytail. Her heart raced with rage, and her thoughts spiraled with the words she wished she would have said to Charlie— more assertions of how little she needed someone like him. "How dare he," she muttered to the kitchen counter. "Classic Manhattan developer guy. Don't know why I expected anything else." The heat from her anger came over her arms and chest; it was almost pleasurable after a season of loss and fear. Anger felt like an emotion she could control.

And she couldn't shake the way Charlie had looked at her as he'd stormed out. The rage in his face had made him even more handsome. It pleased Charlotte, knowing she'd caused that.

"Mom?" Van stepped out of her bedroom with Ethan in her arms and gave Charlotte a nervous smile. "Are you all right?"

Charlotte tried to fix her face. "I'm just fine. How are you feeling?"

"Better." Van frowned, placed Ethan in a bassinet near the kitchen counter, and crossed her arms. Her eyes were more alive than they'd been in previous days. Her mastitis was clearing up. "How did it go with that developer guy?"

"Terribly." Charlotte smiled in spite of herself. "He really infuriated me."

Van laughed. "You look like you just ran a marathon."

"I feel like I just stood up for myself for the first time in a while." Charlotte shook her head. "Everyone should encounter an awful, arrogant man like Charlie Bryant every once in a while. Getting angry at him was my therapy for the year."

"That's good? I guess?" Van blinked at Charlotte with confusion. Then added: "I was thinking we could bake some cookies today. I've been craving them."

That was all Charlotte needed to hear. In a flash, the oven was pre-heated, and she was speckled in flour. Van put Christmas music on the speaker and then used Grandma Dee's Christmas cookie cutters to make reindeer, Christmas trees, Santa Clauses, bells, and snowmen out of the dough. Charlotte snapped the first tray into the oven and clapped her hands. As she'd rolled the dough and hummed along to Christmas tunes, images of long-ago Christmases had come over her. There was her mother, Louise, hovering over Charlotte, helping her cut out a snowman or frost a Santa. There was her mother, telling Charlotte she could taste the dough if she wanted to. But just a little.

"So," Van said, leaning against the counter. "What are

you going to do about the inn now that the developer is out of the picture?"

"I don't know," Charlotte admitted, her stomach twisting. She smeared a bit of the dough onto her finger and tasted it, crunching on the raw sugar.

"Mom! That has raw egg in it," Van scolded her.

Charlotte ignored her. "After we bake the rest of the dough, I have to run."

"Where are you going?" Although she hadn't admitted it, Van was usually nervous when Charlotte left the house for too long. Charlotte was her stand-in partner in all things early motherhood. Charlotte remembered her own fear twenty-eight years ago— as well as her husband's lack of commitment to helping her. She wanted Van to feel supported.

"I won't be gone long. I promise."

Van's face softened. "Are you going to go yell at that developer guy again?"

Charlotte laughed. "I wish. Instead, I have to apologize to my mother, of all people. She's really going to love this. Wish me luck."

* * *

Charlotte wasn't sure of her mother's schedule. According to her grandfather, Louise usually finished her shift at Jeez, Louise by mid-afternoon and returned home to eat a healthy lunch and rest. Sometimes, she returned to the diner for the dinner rush, where she tore her feet and knees apart, serving club sandwiches and French fries.

Louise's house was the same one in which Charlotte had been raised. It was a half-mile from the Cherry Inn and looked exactly the same, with its dark blue shutters and gray siding. Charlotte stood out front with her hands shoved deep in her coat pockets, playing out all the years of her life before her feud with her mother. She could imagine herself walking up and down the walkway, on her way to and from school, skipping, her backpack banging against her. She could imagine herself leaning against the porch, kissing her high school boyfriend good-night. In some ways, this house was even more haunted than the Cherry Inn, heavy with memories. Charlotte swallowed the lump in her throat and forced herself up the walkway. She knocked hard on the door, then craned her ears to hear for movement. But there was nothing.

Like a stalker, Charlotte peered through the front window, wanting to see what the living room looked like. Her mother had gotten a new couch and a new television, but the bookshelf along the side wall was the same as always, and the photograph of Grandma Hank and Grandma Dee on their wedding day hung above the fireplace, just like always. Upon closer inspection, Charlotte realized there was a photograph of Van and Collin as teenagers framed above the couch.

When Charlotte glanced back at the bookshelf, something caught her eye. It seemed impossible. Along the middle shelf were all seven of Charlotte's children's books, which she'd written and illustrated herself. She'd hardly spoken to her mother since that first book about the Cherry Inn had been published. It struck her as bizarre that her mother had gone out of her way to purchase every single one of her books. It was as though, even in her rage, she couldn't overcome her motherly pride.

Charlotte couldn't breathe for a moment. She stared at the children's books, wondering what her mother's opinions of them were. Did she think Charlotte had done a good job? It was suddenly all Charlotte wanted to know in the world.

"Charlotte? Is that you?" A man hollered to Charlotte's right, and Charlotte nearly leaped from her skin.

"Oh! Mr. Velton. Hi." Charlotte stumbled away from the window and waved at Bert Velton, her mother's long-time next-door neighbor. He was shorter than she remembered him, his shoulders stooped, and he wore a thick sweater not dissimilar to Mr. Roger's. His thick glasses made him look vaguely like an adorable turtle.

"I thought that was you." Bert put his hands on his hips and smiled unabashedly from his porch. "Your mother mentioned you were in town."

"Did she?" Charlotte imagined Louise had complained about Charlotte non-stop to anyone who was willing to listen.

"She said she has a new great-grandson," Bert said.

"My daughter had a baby. Ethan." Charlotte's voice cracked with love.

"I hope you'll bring him by soon!" Bert went on. "I know your mother wants to dote on him. She's such a baby lover."

Charlotte furrowed her brow. Her mother? A baby lover? To Charlotte, Louise was an angry woman, ready to hurl an insult in your direction whenever she got the chance. It was difficult to imagine her doting over a baby.

Then again, the Louise in Charlotte's deepest memories had been so soft and kind. To Charlotte, she'd been a loving and beautiful queen.

"Anyway, if you're looking for your mother, she's at the diner," Bert went on. "She said it's been really busy there this week. There are lots of folks from out of town wanting the magic of a small town at Christmas. I suppose you, being from the city, can understand that."

Charlotte walked slowly to the Jeez, Louise diner, feeling a mix of dread and excitement. The Louise she'd just heard about from Bert didn't sound anything like the woman who'd stormed into the apartment the other day and screamed at her. She was curious to meet that other Louise, but she wasn't sure Louise would ever reveal that side of herself. Perhaps too much had happened between them.

Just as Bert had warned, when Charlotte approached the Jeez, Louise diner, she found it in a state of chaos. Every single booth, stool, and table was taken, filled to the brim with Christmas shoppers and Christmas revelers, most of whom looked to be from the city. In the center of it all was Louise, her hair in a wild mess behind her as she rushed from table to table. She'd always prided herself on never needing to write any of the orders down, but through the window, Charlotte could see her mother was struggling, muttering to herself as a way to remember what people wanted. Behind the counter, Charlotte could see the fry cooks and other kitchen staff members running themselves ragged in the kitchen, spitting out delicious, greasy diner food. Charlotte's stomach rumbled. All she'd had that afternoon was cookie dough— a rookie mistake.

Back in middle school and high school, even long before Charlotte had legally been able to work, Charlotte had worked at the Jeez, Louise diner. She and her mother had worked tirelessly, shift after shift, slinging plates, fetching drinks, taking orders, and slicing pieces of pie. As a result, Charlotte had developed her mother's miraculous memory. In college, she'd impressed her friends by memorizing entire Shakespeare sonnets and Edgar Allen Poe poems.

Now, Charlotte knew what she had to do. She pressed open the door of the diner, making the bell jingle overhead. Her mother was too busy with a table and didn't glance her way. Charlotte removed her coat, breezed past the counter, fetched an apron, and waved hello to one of the fry cooks, a guy named Calvin who'd been there for years.

Charlotte hurried up to a table that hadn't been served yet— a family who looked glum, their children kicking each other under the table. "Sorry about your wait," Charlotte said. "Can I get you started on drinks?"

"We can order everything now," the father said with a sniff. He wore a shirt with a high thread count, something that had probably cost upwards of two hundred dollars. They looked like Upper East Side money.

"I'm ready for you," Charlotte said, maintaining her smile.

Suddenly, her mother's breath was hot on the back of her neck. "What are you doing here?" She sounded even angrier than she'd been at the apartment.

"What can I get you?" Charlotte asked the man, ignoring her mother.

Her mother's hands flew up as she scurried past to fill glasses with water. Her face was beet red. Charlotte concentrated hard on the man's order, a collection of burgers, soups, sandwiches, and salads, plus coffees, a diet soda, and a regular soda. The Jeez, Louise diner wasn't updated with modern technology (obviously), which meant there was no computer for inputting orders into the kitchen. The Jeez, Louise Diner would never waste money on such a system. Charlotte scribbled the order on a piece of paper that she handed to one of the fry cooks and got to work on the drinks. As she filled one of the glasses with regular soda, her mother appeared beside her and grumbled, "I don't need your help."

Just then, another family of five entered the diner, the bell jangling overhead. Charlotte turned on her heel and said, "Welcome to the Jeez, Louise diner! The wait for the next table is about ten minutes. Can we get you something to drink while you wait?"

Louise flared her nostrils and gaped at Charlotte. As the family of five grabbed menus, Louise lowered her voice and added, "I know you're too good for this now. Don't pretend like you care. It makes it so much worse."

Charlotte shot her mother a look. "Tables six and seven are still waiting to order. Table ten looks like they want to pay. We can get them out of here and seat that new table. What do you say?"

Louise waffled between what looked like incredulity and anger. With a final sigh, she whirled around and headed for table ten to take their money. Charlotte fixed her smile, brought the drinks to the Upper East Side family, and took table six and table seven's orders. Already, she felt herself a part of the flow of the diner. As long as they kept moving, they would get through this rush. The diner was just as it always had been, as was waitressing. She felt both forty-eight and seventeen at once.

But Bert hadn't been lying. White Plains was awash with tourists, all of whom had, apparently, been told that the Jeez, Louise diner offered the very best food in the area.

"A friend of ours told us to come here," the father from the Upper East Side said happily as he passed Charlotte a wad of cash. "And she was right. This was the pinnacle of the small-town experience. We have another group of friends coming out here in a few days. We'll be sure to recommend."

Charlotte's knees had begun to ache from whipping around the dining room. "I'm so glad to hear that."

For the next three and a half hours, nearly every table in the diner was taken. One of the kitchen staffers had to run to the grocery store to buy more bread and butter. Other kitchen staff members threatened to start smoking again; such was their stress. "Don't do it, Johnny!" Charlotte cried as she headed toward a table laden with plates.

Although Louise hadn't verbalized it, it seemed she'd accepted the fact that she needed Charlotte, at least for now. They'd begun to communicate better, with Louise asking Charlotte to take over a table while she dealt with a bill, or Charlotte cleaning up a soda spill as Louise cleaned a few tables for newcomers, and so on. Partially, Charlotte wanted to prove to her mother that she didn't think she was "better" than the diner; partially, it was fun. Charlotte had spent the majority of her professional career hidden away at a desk, writing children's books. There was something to be said for walking around, talking to people, and feeling a part of the world. She understood why her mother loved it so.

At five, miraculously, the diner cleared. Louise gasped and raced for the door, where she turned the closed sign to face outward.

"I can't take it anymore," she announced. "We aren't doing dinner. They can all go somewhere else."

In the kitchen, the staffers howled with relief and set to work on clean-up. Charlotte and Louise collapsed in stools along the counter and stared straight ahead, drinking ice water. Charlotte had decided to wait for her mother to speak first. Louise had seemingly decided to take a vow of silence. Perhaps they would sit like this all night, avoiding each other's gaze. Then again, Charlotte needed to get back to Van and the baby soon.

After three of the kitchen staffers said, "*good night*," Louise cleared her throat and said, "I guess thanks are in order." Her tone was dismissal. It was probably the best Charlotte could hope for. She reminded herself of all seven of her children's books, collected together on the middle shelf in her mother's living room.

"It was fun," Charlotte offered.

Louise's face stiffened. "I'm sure it's fun for you. It's not your livelihood."

Charlotte wanted to roll her eyes so badly, but miraculously, she didn't. "Listen," Charlotte said, "I have to get back to Van. She's so anxious with the new baby, and she likes it when I'm around."

Louise's cheek twitched. "Then you'd better run home."

"Why don't you come with me?" Charlotte pushed her luck. "We made Christmas cookies this afternoon, and we need help decorating them. I know how good you are at that."

"You don't need to flatter me."

"I'm not. Trust me." Charlotte chewed her lower lip, marveling at the stubbornness of her mother. Finally, she said, "I came here to apologize, you know."

Louise's eyes widened.

"I had no idea what you were talking about the other day," Charlotte went on. "When you stormed into the apartment. But then, I met with the developer I'd discussed the Cherry Inn with. He showed me his designs. His ideas. I realized you'd seen them."

Louise clenched her jaw.

"Obviously, I told him to go back where he came from," Charlotte said with a laugh. "I thought he was going to restore the spirit of the old place, not completely destroy it."

Charlotte wanted to tell her mother that she wasn't rich and famous and that she was more-or-less a very lonely and middle-class writer. But she didn't want to push her luck, not now that her mother seemed to look at her differently, with more respect.

"Come back with me," Charlotte said. "Let's have a glass of wine and some cookies and talk about what to do with the inn. At first, I thought it was best to flip it and sell it, but there has to be a way to save it. I love that place too much to give it up."

Louise shook her head sadly. "I don't know how. But you're right. We have to try."

Chapter Eleven

C harlie continued drawing the plans for the Cherry Inn. He threw himself into the details, staying up late at night, sharpening his pencil and putting more logs on the fire. Although he'd heard Charlotte tell him she never wanted to see him again, that she hated the designs, he wasn't accustomed to being told "no." He believed in what he'd drawn. And he genuinely believed Charlotte would come around, call him out of the blue, and ask him to come back to the Cherry Inn to start anew. "Everyone knows how talented you are," Sarah had told him so often. "You just have to wait for them to realize what's right in front of them."

Three days after Charlie's big fight with Charlotte at the Cherry Inn, there was a knock at the cabin. Charlie was drinking coffee by the fire, going over his recent drawings. His first thought was that this was Charlotte coming to tell him how wrong she'd been. Maybe he'd tell her he'd decided not to work with her anymore— that she'd missed her chance. Or maybe he'd tell her she was the most beautiful woman he'd met in years, and the thought of their argument kept him awake at night. His heart raced.

But when Charlie opened the door, he found himself face-to-face with his assistant, Timothy. Timothy was pale and thinner than he'd been when Charlie had left the city. Behind him in the parking lot was Timothy's Prius.

"Timothy!" Charlie was so surprised to see him that he forgot to be angry. "Good afternoon!"

Timothy bristled. "Good afternoon?"

"Come in! Would you like coffee? A sandwich?"

Timothy followed Charlie into the cabin and glanced around the single room with distrustful eyes. Charlie realized he'd never seen Timothy outside the context of a swanky Manhattan boardroom, office, or cocktail party. Timothy didn't fit the mold of the cabin.

"This is where you've been?" Timothy asked.

"Yes," Charlie said simply. He passively wondered how Timothy had found him. Then again, Timothy had access to nearly everything in Charlie's life, including his calendars and his bank accounts. It probably hadn't been so hard to track him down.

"Can I ask why?" Timothy asked, his voice breaking.

Charlie laughed openly, surprised at how happy he felt. Normally, when he spoke with Timothy, he felt as though his heart was several different pieces put back together with scotch tape. Perhaps it was the forest air, or it was the new project. But he felt like a new man.

"Right in the middle of the most important party of your career thus far," Timothy went on. "You just left?"

Charlie raised his shoulders.

"And Baxter Bailey seems to think you're out of the city, working on the next big project?" Timothy went on.

"So, I've been telling him everything is going really well? And that you're nearly ready to bring him in?"

Charlie's smile fell. "You told him what?"

"I didn't want him to lose faith in you," Timothy said. "I wanted him to think that whatever you were doing, you were thinking of him, too."

Charlie turned slowly, puffed out his cheeks, and stared out the window. His decades-long relationship with Baxter Bailey was a blessing and a curse. There was no way Charlie could have made it so long in his career without Baxter— and yet now, the idea of seeing Baxter again made Charlie feel on the verge of throwing up.

"I'm not ready to loop Baxter into this project yet," Charlie said, his tone dark.

Timothy sighed, clearly disgruntled. "He needed answers, Charlie. I had to answer for you."

"What do you mean?"

"I mean that he's on his way here," Timothy said.

Charlie turned and glared at Timothy. He wanted to remind Timothy that he'd sent him a sizeable bonus for Christmas. All Timothy had had to do over the next few weeks was kick back and relax with his wife and children. What would Charlie give to be able to do the same? Everything. He would have given everything.

But there was no use arguing. If Baxter Bailey was on the way to see Charlie, Charlie couldn't call him off. He had to pretend as though the entire trip to White Plains had really all been about his and Baxter Bailey's continued commitment to one another.

Charlie wore a false smile. He felt suddenly, horribly tired— just as tired as he'd felt in the minutes before he'd decided to escape Manhattan. Manhattan had caught up to him.

"Why don't you head back to the city, Timothy?" he suggested. "Maybe you've done enough for today."

Timothy was very pale. He stuttered, saying, "I want you to know that I really..."

But Charlie had no interest in hearing what Timothy had to say. He walked around him and opened the door, ushering him out. "Have a safe drive back," he said. "I have to prep for a big business meeting. Isn't that what you want?"

With Timothy gone, Charlie sat back in his chair by the fire and rubbed his eyes. He wanted to pretend Timothy's visit had been a nightmare, just something he'd concocted during his afternoon nap, but Timothy's cologne still lingered in the air— something ridiculously expensive and reeking of patchouli.

Three hours after Timothy left came the crunch of the tires in the snow out front. Charlie stood to answer the door, watching as Baxter stepped from his Lamborghini and raised a hand in greeting. Charlie had the feeling of having been hunted; as though he were a cornered deer.

"This place is really something!" Baxter said as he approached the cabin. "A rugged cabin for the intellectual genius. Who are you? Thoreau?" He clapped Charlie's shoulder and entered the cabin without Charlie saying anything. He acted as though he owned Charlie. Perhaps, in a way, he did.

"Wow." Baxter leaned against the wooden countertop and shook his head, inspecting the room. He looked fascinated, unlike Timothy, who'd just looked disgusted. "When Timothy told me where you'd gone, I said, 'White Plains? New Jersey?' I couldn't believe it. But now, I do. I really, really do."

Charlie poured them both glasses of whiskey, the grocery store brand he'd bought downtown. Baxter howled with laughter after it touched his lips.

"This is like gasoline!"

Charlie smiled. "The grocery store in town doesn't have many options."

"I imagine not." Baxter inhaled the full shot and refilled his glass. "Charming. Just charming." He took another shot. "Timothy has me all excited about your next project, Charlie. I drove out here with this feeling that we were about to take on the world together, you and me. It's not another useless Manhattan project. It's not another boring apartment building. But something real! Something historical!"

Charlie's smile was half genuine now. "I didn't realize that's what you wanted."

"Desperately," Baxter said. "I want to feel a part of something. And when I drove through White Plains just now, I realized this place has a story deep in its bones. It's the people who care about it; they decorate it head to toe for Christmas, and they ask one another how they are over coffee at the diner. That's why city folks like us come out here. We want to feel that heartbeat."

Charlie wasn't sure if Baxter was spouting poetry to manipulate him. Perhaps Baxter was cleverer than Charlie gave him credit for. Although he wasn't a self-made billionaire, he'd made a series of well-timed choices that Charlie couldn't turn up his nose at.

"So," Baxter said, clapping his hands. "When will you show me your vision? When can I see the newest Charlie Bryant original?"

Charlie led Baxter to the designs on his desk. Baxter sat down before them, put on his reading glasses, and scoured the pages, moving each aside delicately. Charlie leaned against the wall throughout, watching the fire die out across the logs. He felt too exhausted to sustain the blaze. Somehow, in showing Baxter his newest passion project, he felt as though he was tainting it.

After more than twenty-five minutes of silence, Baxter raised his head and blinked at Charlie. He looked mesmerized.

"This is sensational." Baxter was very quiet. "Truly. It steeps old-world charm with modern luxuries."

Charlie had said basically the same thing to Charlotte. He hated remembering this now. Was he just as soulless as Baxter?

"It's genius to tear out that wall on the second floor," Baxter went on. "And I just love these shower concepts. The waterfalls? The jacuzzis? They're gorgeous. The guests will go bananas for them."

Charlie nodded. He'd thought the same.

"Tell me," Baxter said, removing his glasses. "How do the current owners feel about this?"

"They're coming around to it," Charlie lied.

Baxter grinned. "They're resistant, I suppose?"

Charlie raised his shoulders. "It doesn't fully align with their memories."

Baxter laughed. "I imagine not. People are nostalgic, aren't they? Well, I'm willing to put down a very, very kind offer."

"It needs a lot of work." Charlie wasn't sure if he wanted to chase Baxter away from the idea or lure him closer.

"My offer stands," Baxter said.

Charlie was quiet for a moment, imagining himself telling Charlotte about the money. This would be money for her daughter, her grandson, her grandfather, and whoever else she cared about— enough to change their lives forever. She just had to stop being so stubborn.

But wasn't Charlotte's stubbornness one of the reasons he couldn't get her out of his head? She was unlike anyone he'd met in years.

"Listen, Charlie." Baxter's smile wavered. "I'm an honest man. As honest as they come in the business world, at least. And for that reason, I want to acknowledge what I know to be true."

Charlie maintained eye contact.

"You tried to run away. You don't have to own up to it. I already know. You fled the city and everyone in it as though it were on fire," Baxter went on, speaking casually. "And I think I know why. You want a life like this. Peace and quiet. Time to whittle or whistle or whatever it is you creative people do. And if you close this deal with the Cherry Inn, I can promise you many more months here, just like this. Once we re-open the Cherry Inn, we'll be able to capitalize on all those city folks eager for a breath of fresh air. And maybe you can find another inn to flip after that. What do you say?"

Charlie's throat was tight. He'd grown to suspect that making deals with Baxter Bailey was a bit like making deals with the devil. There was always a catch.

But Baxter knew what Charlie wanted. Charlie had all the money in the world, and now, he just wanted time to work and time to think. More than that, he wanted time to mourn— and to punish himself for what he'd done. And he just couldn't do that in the city.

Charlie's hand shook as he extended it. "I'll convince them to sell."

Baxter's smile was enormous. "I always knew you

were my guy," he said. "Ever since I first met you. I knew you'd change my life."

Baxter convinced Charlie to go out with him after that. He wanted to celebrate their "newfound commitment" to one another. Charlie couldn't think of an excuse not to go. Because Rudy's was the only bar in town, Charlie found himself elbow to elbow with Baxter at Rudy's bar-top, clinking glasses of the best scotch they had. Rudy eyed him from the corner of the bar, drying a beer glass with his head tilted. Charlie felt his judgment—he understood what he looked like, seated next to this well-dressed billionaire in a dive bar. But when Charlie raised his glass toward Rudy, Rudy smiled and nodded back. It was as though he understood the chaos that whirled in Charlie's mind. Maybe that was the magic of bartenders. They were a bit like therapists and psychics all rolled into one.

"To your new life in this two-bit town," Baxter said. "And to my next pay day. Who would have thought it would have come out of a place like White Plains? I guess life can still surprise me."

Chapter Twelve

In the wake of their reunion at the Jeez, Louse diner, Louise and Charlotte continued to hit roadblocks in their relationship. It wasn't like they could go from not speaking for years to a loving mother-daughter relationship with the snap of their fingers. That wasn't how people worked— and it certainly wasn't how Louise Summers operated. Louise still found ways to poke and prod Charlotte, to remind Charlotte of her anger and brokenness. Charlotte was surprisingly resilient, able to brush off her mother's comments, reminding herself of her mother's tremendously painful life. Perhaps because of Charlotte's continued commitment, Louise appeared on the doorstep of the apartment nearly every day. Her excuse was simple. Apparently, it had nothing to do with Charlotte. Louise wanted to hold the baby.

Miraculously, Louise had listened to Charlotte's advice to hire more people to work at the diner. Twenty-somethings who needed extra shifts for their expenses during the Christmas season ambled in and were given the job immediately. When they asked Louise where the computer was and why the diner didn't take credit cards, Louise glowered at them until they apologized and put on their aprons.

On a morning when she wasn't needed at the diner, a rarity in Louise Summers' life, Louise ambled up the back entrance of the apartment, wiped her boots on the welcome mat, and drew Van into a hug. Charlotte was in the La-Z-Boy, rocking Ethan, who had just eaten and fallen back to sleep.

"Shoot. I missed him again, didn't I?" Louise sighed with adoration and cupped her hands together. "Look at how sweet he is! Van, you created a perfect baby."

Van laughed. "Can I get you a cup of coffee, Grandma?"

Louise agreed and sat on the island in the kitchen, her eyes still on Ethan. Charlotte felt a great amount of power in taking care of her grandson. He needed her so completely. He was helpless.

"So, Grandma," Van said as she placed a mug of coffee on the counter. "Mom and I were thinking we'd get started on the inn today."

Louise cocked her eyebrow. "Get started? What do you mean?"

Charlotte smiled. Her heart fluttered with nerves. "We're going to clean it out. See how bad the damage is."

"Maybe it just needs a bit of dusting," Van suggested.

"I sincerely doubt that." Louise sipped her coffee.

"We want to do it," Charlotte assured her. "No matter what we decide to do with it, it needs some TLC."

"If you want to waste your time, be my guest," Louise said.

Although she gave excuse after excuse and complained for nearly a full ten minutes, Louise eventually agreed to help out with the inn's initial clean-up. "But only so I can hold Ethan next time he wakes up," she insisted as she retrieved the vacuum from the hall closet.

"You can even feed him next," Van assured her.

Charlotte, Van, and Louise set to work on the main floor of the inn. They relieved the furniture of its white sheets, vacuumed corners, and cleaned windows until they glinted. It seemed there was probably a mice problem, to which Van suggested they buy no-kill traps. "No kill?" Louise asked, as though she'd never heard of anything so ridiculous in her life. "I can't bear to kill them, Grandma," Van told her. "Those are my terms, and I'm sticking to them." They mopped the hardwood, made lists of supplies they needed to buy, and dusted the cubby holes, where they found the old iron keys, still waiting for new guests.

"When was the last time Grandpa had any guests?" Charlotte asked.

"Ten years?" Louise suggested. "Something like that."

Charlotte knew her mother was just pretending not to know. Louise had a record of everything in that head of hers and could have probably told her the exact date and time the final guest checked out. It was part of the reason she struggled so much with forgiveness.

After nearly three hours of cleaning, Ethan wailed, and Van and Louise hurried to tend to him. "I have a bottle ready for him, Grandma," Van said.

Louise's eyes glinted with excitement. Charlotte understood that after so many years, she was needed in this very acute, biological way. There was nothing like feeding a baby.

Together, Louise and Van re-entered the apartment, leaving Charlotte in the creaking shadows of the inn. She finished mopping the dining room, feeling slick with sweat yet still chilly due to the drafts of the old place. They needed a roaring fire in the fireplace, like old times. They needed a Christmas tree.

But after just three hours of work, the downstairs was beginning to look okay. Clean, anyway. Modest. No, it wasn't state-of-the-art luxury like in Charlie's designs. And it probably wasn't good enough to advertise for new guests. But Charlotte could sit on the floor of the living room in front of the fireplace, close her eyes, and almost imagine she was eight years old and that her grandfather was preparing to tell her and her cousins his Christmas story again. Almost.

Suddenly, there was a knock at the front door. Charlotte's eyes popped open, and she found herself in the year 2023— not 1983.

But who was at the door?

Charlotte hurried toward the foyer, inspecting the now-dusted front desk with pride. This was her family's greatest joy and a final link to her Grandma Dee. It was time they treated it with respect.

To Charlotte's surprise, on the other side of the door was Charlie Bryant. He wore a thick pea coat, and his black and gray hair was ruffled into curls from the sharp winter wind. From the look of his red face, he'd walked through the woods between the cabin and downtown again.

Charlotte had a wild urge to throw the door back into his face.

"Afternoon," Charlie said. His smile stopped Charlotte in her tracks. She'd forgotten how handsome he was.

"Hello?" Charlotte glowered at him. Probably, she looked just as cruel as her mother.

"I wanted to come by and apologize," Charlie said.

Charlotte stiffened. She hadn't imagined a city-guy like Charlie to be so kind and free-wheeling with his apologies. What was the catch?

"You don't need to apologize," Charlotte said, beginning to close the door. "We've already said all we need to say. Don't you think?"

"I just think we got off on the wrong foot," Charlie interjected.

Charlotte cocked her head. Something about the way he looked at her made her keep the door open, and sharp winter wind blasted against her face. Maybe she was a fool. Scratch that. She was definitely a fool.

"Listen," Charlie went on. "I just walked past this little Christmas market downtown. There are food stalls and mulled wine."

"It's there every year," Charlotte said.

"I'm sure it is. But it's nothing like we get in the city," Charlie went on. "Would you like a mug of mulled wine? Or hot chocolate? On me, of course. As an apology."

Charlotte didn't know what to make of this. She flinched, wanting to run back into the apartment and tend to baby Ethan. But Louise and Van had Ethan's needs covered. And it was true that she loved mulled wine, especially drinking it as the snow fell as it was now, softly and magically, as though they lived in the glowing orb of a snow globe.

"I'm sure you could find someone else to drink mulled wine with," Charlotte protested, glancing down at her jeans, which were scuffed at the knee with dust and grime from the inn.

"I don't know anyone else in this town," Charlie

reminded her. "Please. Don't let me drink mulled wine alone."

* * *

Charlie waited for Charlotte in the foyer of the Cherry Inn while she breezed back to the apartment to change clothes. Louise was in Van's room, giving Ethan a bottle, and he was looking at her, his eyes shining. Van monitored Louise in the corner, her arms over her chest, as though she struggled to let anyone else do what she was biologically programmed to do— care for her baby. But Charlotte knew this was healing for Louise. Van understood that, too.

"I'm heading out for a second," Charlotte hissed to her mother and Van.

"I won't be here when you get back," Louise said, not bothering to glance Charlotte's way.

"Thank you for your help today," Charlotte offered. "We couldn't have gotten so much done without you."

Charlotte changed into a pair of fleece tights, a black dress, a pair of black boots, and a thick, fuzzy hat. After she donned her winter coat, she applied a very soft shade of pink lipstick. She didn't want to look as though she was trying too hard. But, even if she and Charlie ended up fighting again, she wanted to look fiery and beautiful. She wanted to feel like the sort of woman who could date a man like Charlie, even if it was the last thing in the world she wanted to do.

When Charlotte returned to the foyer to collect Charlie, he looked taken aback for a moment. Charlotte touched her face, fearful she'd smeared her lipstick.

"Is there something wrong?"

"Nothing at all," Charlie said. "Shall we?"

They walked down Main Street, headed toward the courthouse, before which they'd set up the annual Christmas Market. Little red food stalls were dotted throughout the square, and Christmas lights were strung overhead, glinting against the dying light of the very late afternoon.

"It looks like a fairy tale," Charlie said.

"I genuinely thought it was when I was a kid. I grew up in White Plains, but it always transformed at Christmastime. It felt like a completely different place for a few weeks."

Charlie smiled at her. Charlotte wanted to scold herself for telling him such intimate details about her childhood.

"My assistant called me from Manhattan this morning," Charlie said. "And through the phone, I heard all these honks and beeps and screeching tires." He wrinkled his nose.

"You've been living in that cabin all alone, like a Buddhist monk," Charlotte joked. "You're going to forget how to live amongst the rest of us soon."

Charlie laughed openly. "I'm approaching enlightenment."

"If you find it, can you tell us how to reach it?" Charlotte asked. "We're floundering here."

In line for mulled wine, Charlotte was surprised at how easily their conversation continued to flow. They bantered about Buddhism, about chess, and about their favorite hole-in-the-wall Chinese restaurants in Manhattan— many of which overlapped.

"You won't get good Chinese out here," Charlotte said as she held her mug with both hands.

"It's a price I'm willing to pay," Charlie said. "Cheers."

Charlotte and Charlie wandered through the Christmas stalls, commenting on local artisans' knitted hats, gloves, and sweaters, the wooden carvings of a local craftsman, and the clay pots and plates fired in a kiln not far from White Plains. Charlotte pondered for a long time about whether to get her mother a beautiful plum-colored vase, then returned it and gave Charlie a funny smile.

"You met my mother, you know."

Charlie raised his eyebrows. "Did I?"

"At the diner."

Charlie placed his hand over his mouth. "Your mother is Jeez, Louise?"

"She is," Charlotte said, shaking with laughter.

"She saw the drawings." Charlie looked as though he'd just solved an impossible riddle.

Charlotte waved her hand. "Don't worry about it. She knows I said no to you. In a way, it weirdly brought us back together."

"I never saw myself as the type to reunite families."

"How do you see yourself?" Charlotte took another sip of hot, tangy wine.

"Good question," Charlie said. "In Buddhism, there is no self."

Charlotte rolled her eyes. "Seriously! Come on. How do you see yourself?"

Charlie looked uncomfortable, as though she'd just accused him of committing a crime. He cast his eyes across the small crowd of the Christmas market, which was mostly city-folks, here to experience small-town Christmas.

"I see myself as a businessman," Charlie said finally. "That probably sounds sad to you, doesn't it?"

"It doesn't matter what I think," Charlotte said.

Charlie nodded. "I don't like seeing myself that way. It's part of the reason I came out here. I wanted a different context." He smiled distractedly, his eyes still elsewhere. "I wanted to remember how I used to see myself. I wanted to see if there was any of him leftover."

This tugged at Charlotte's heartstrings. Yet again, Charlie Bryant had surprised her.

"Have you found him at all?" Charlotte asked. "Your past self, I mean."

Charlie shrugged. "Sometimes, when I'm deep in the woods, I close my eyes and pretend to be him. I imagine I'm twenty-four, still in the suburbs of Chicago. Still broke. Still so unsure of where my life was going to go."

Charlotte couldn't believe how open Charlie was. It felt as though they'd carved out another dimension for themselves, where they could speak clearly and honestly about their souls.

Of course, this wasn't a date. But if it had been, Charlotte would have chosen this moment to fall head-over-heels in love.

Suddenly, Charlie dropped his head down to whisper in Charlotte's ear. "Isn't that your mom?"

Charlotte's heartbeat raced. She followed Charlie's gaze across the Christmas Market to find her mother, all bundled up and smiling. Like Charlotte, she'd opted for lipstick, but hers was brighter red, more scandalous. What was she laughing at? Charlotte followed Louise's eyes to a dark figure beside her, with grizzled hair and a thick, dark coat. Charlotte grabbed Charlie's elbow.

"That's her neighbor!" Charlotte breathed. "Bert Velton!"

"That's Bert Velton?" Charlie gasped.

Charlotte turned to lock eyes with Charlie. "How do you know about Bert?"

Charlie laughed. "I don't. I just love how excited you look right now."

Charlotte tugged Charlie's elbow and led him around the side of a Christmas stall. "My mother is on a date," she whispered. "I can't believe it."

"She looks beautiful," Charlie said. "That lipstick is something special."

"My mother never wears lipstick like that," Charlotte said. "And as far as I know, she hasn't been on a date in years."

"Didn't you say you weren't in contact for a while?"

Charlotte grimaced. It was true: there was so little she really knew of her mother's current life. She filled her mouth with more mulled wine.

"My father left when we were really little," Charlotte offered. "And my mother spent most of my childhood telling me that men weren't worth anything."

Charlotte could have told Charlie that Louise hadn't spoken to Charlotte after she'd married someone she didn't like; she could have told him that her ex turned out to be exactly as Louise had said he was.

But Charlie Bryant was just Charlie Bryant, a handsome developer from Manhattan. He wasn't her secret-keeper.

"It looks like she thinks Bert is worth something," Charlie teased. "I wish someone looked at me the way Louise looks at him."

Charlotte punched Charlie's upper arm lightly,

surprised at how flirtatious she felt. It was as though there were bubbles in her chest, getting bigger and bursting. "If she sees me, she'll get distracted and upset," Charlotte admitted. "And I don't want her to think I'm in cahoots with you again."

Charlie's cheeks were slack. He looked disappointed. Charlotte suddenly felt as though disappointing Charlie was the very last thing she wanted to do in the world.

And then, she heard herself say, "But we could get some food, maybe. There's an Italian restaurant that isn't half-bad. Here in town, we say the owner is the daughter of an old mob boss back in the city. But that's just gossip."

Charlie's eyes brightened. Perhaps he just didn't want to be left alone in his cabin anymore. And perhaps Charlotte wanted to continue this conversation. Was that a crime?

"Let's do it," Charlie said.

"Great," Charlotte said. She was suddenly famished from cleaning up the inn, and she wanted to inhale mounds of pasta and red sauce. She wanted to order a half-carafe of wine and clink her glass with Charlie's. She wanted to hear more of his confessions. "But it's not a date," she said as they wandered through the snow. "In case that wasn't clear."

"Buddhists don't date," Charlie assured her with a joking smile. "It's the furthest thing from my mind."

Chapter Thirteen

Christmas 2020

The apartment in Greenwich Village was four times the size of the apartment Sarah and Charlie had started out in. The price was astronomical, a number Sarah refused to say aloud as she felt it was cursed. They signed for it on December 1st, then stepped into a snowy Manhattan, hand-in-hand, ready to waste the afternoon together.

At a coffee shop around the corner from the new place, Charlie ordered them cappuccinos and a croissant to share, then joined Sarah at the window. Sarah was now forty-two, a sought-after immigration lawyer, and a fashionista in the truest sense. After she'd been able to abandon the wardrobe she'd had back in Chicago, made up of second-hand clothes and hand-me-downs, she'd built up a wardrobe of sleek pantsuits, gorgeous dresses, and high heels. Sometimes, she joked, "If only my past self could see me now. She would cry."

Charlie and Sarah clinked their cappuccino mugs

together and held the silence. They'd wanted to move out of their apartment near Chinatown for many years; it was finally happening. This was the next stage of their life.

"Melissa just texted," Sarah said. "Theater practice was canceled today."

"So, we'll pick her up early?" Charlie was unabashedly pleased.

"At three," Sarah said. "I can't wait to tell her about the apartment."

"Do you think it'll make her consider staying in the city after graduation?" Charlie asked.

Sarah's eyes clouded. "What is it about California? I don't get it. New York has everything! And we're here. She could live in Greenwich Village and go to NYU. It's basically a dream come true."

"But she wants to carve her own path," Charlie said. "We were the same way."

Sarah rubbed her temples. "Maybe we can bribe her to stay."

Charlie laughed. He wasn't accustomed to his wife manipulating their daughter. Throughout Melissa's childhood, he and Sarah had had endless conversations about helping her become "the woman she was meant to be," about ensuring she had confidence and that she knew how to speak her mind. Sarah had spoken about being raised to be quiet, to be meek. To always apologize. They didn't want their daughter to make herself smaller just because society demanded it.

"I'm kidding, of course," Sarah said.

"Of course," Charlie said. He kissed Sarah on the cheek, and his chest felt heavy, pressurized with too much love.

Charlie and Sarah met Melissa outside the gate of

Melissa's high school. Melissa scrambled toward them. She was tall for her age, with long arms and legs and dark blonde hair in a stream behind her. She hugged them and asked, "Well? Did you do it?"

"We got the apartment!" Sarah cried, cupping Melissa's elbows.

Melissa screeched and jumped up and down happily. "It's gorgeous! I cannot wait!"

The plan was to move into the apartment after New Year's Eve. Charlie had turned down several developer jobs that autumn and winter, bent on setting up his new apartment and taking time with his daughter during her final year of high school. It was impossible to him just how quickly life had gone. One minute, he and Sarah had been struggling to make ends meet in Chicago, and the next, he was arm-in-arm with the billionaire Baxter Bailey, working on some of the most iconic projects in the city. Melissa had been a toddler, and then suddenly, she'd been seventeen.

As they decorated the Christmas tree that night in their apartment near Chinatown, Charlie announced his plans to Sarah and Melissa. "A road trip. We'll do a big circle through New England, hit up all the small towns for their Christmas charm, and maybe even make time for Niagara Falls."

Sarah smiled knowingly. She remembered that first road trip so many years ago when she'd told Charlie about the baby. They wouldn't return to that motel room at the edges of White Plains, New Jersey, of course. But they could rent a nice vacation spot somewhere near there and reminisce.

"We have to make a list of road trip snacks," Melissa announced. "Twizzlers are a must. Pretzels. Doritos." She counted them out on her fingers, her eyes illuminated. It occurred to Charlie that his daughter hadn't had a childhood like his; she'd hardly spent much time in a car, whereas he'd continually been in his mother's car, whiling away the hours. Probably, Melissa thought of road trips with romanticism. She'd also read *On the Road* by Jack Kerouac that year; maybe that had something to do with it.

"We'll make Christmas cookies," Sarah added.

"Great idea, Mom," Melissa said. "I can't wait to get out of the city!"

Later, after Melissa disappeared into her bedroom to text her friends, Charlie and Sarah poured themselves glasses of wine and cozied up on the couch. They laughed about Melissa's desire to leave the city when all Sarah and Charlie had done was fight to get into it.

"Children always push back against their parents," Sarah said. "Even kids as perfect as Melissa."

Charlie and Sarah had secretly wanted more children. They'd tried continually in the years after Melissa's birth, praying for a miracle. But the doctors said that Sarah shouldn't have gotten pregnant in the first place— there was something wrong with her cervix. They'd decided to throw all the love in the world Melissa's way. They couldn't regret that.

The day after Melissa's school let out for the holidays, Charlie, Sarah, and Melissa loaded up the Volvo and got on the road. It wasn't far to White Plains, just a two-hour hop into northern New Jersey, but the contrast between the city and the outskirts was like night and day. Very soon, they were shrouded on either side by deep, impenetrable woods.

"I just saw three deer!" Melissa cried from the backseat. "They were running through the trees! I could see their white tails!"

"Three, huh? Okay. Melissa is winning. Sarah, we have to try to keep up."

"I didn't know this was a contest," Sarah joked.

"Everything is a contest in this family," Charlie said. "You should know that!" Between the seats, he and Sarah held hands, and his heartbeat felt very slow and solid. He felt as though he was exactly where he was supposed to be.

The vacation house he'd booked on the outskirts of White Plains had once been a farmhouse. It towered over the fields beside it and was flanked with thick woods. The barn was painted a bright red and was used for wedding festivities, while the house itself had been completely remodeled on the inside, allowing guests to enjoy an indoor sauna, pool, hot tub, a movie theater, two different kitchens, and beds comfier than anything he and Sarah had ever experienced.

"You have to ask them the brand," Sarah said as she rolled around on the mattress. "We have to buy them for the new apartment. One in every room!"

Charlie dropped onto the mattress beside her, placed his hand on her stomach, and kissed her with his eyes closed. From down the hall came Melissa's cry: "Have you seen the showers? They're like waterfalls!"

Charlie, Sarah, and Melissa went downstairs to assess the kitchen. There, they brewed hot chocolate with marshmallows and sat in the nook, watching the snowfall across the fields and over the woods.

"I don't hear anything," Melissa whispered, shaking her head. "It's like the city doesn't even exist."

Sarah and Charlie locked eyes across the table. Charlie felt a strange pang of regret. Should he have raised his daughter out of the chaos of the city? Perhaps all children just really craved nature.

Melissa decided she wanted to go for a walk. They bundled up in boots, snow pants, coats, hats, and gloves and crunched across the rolling hills, headed for the woods. Above them, cardinals flitted in and out of the trees, and several fat gray squirrels regarded them from tree branches, too big to run away. Melissa took photographs of everything with her cell phone, wanting to document their big trip away. Everything she said and everything she did, Charlie wanted to write down for himself. In a year, Melissa would be in California, so far away. He and Sarah would be heartbroken. They would need their memories.

For a long time, Melissa ordered that they stand behind a tree, watching three large rabbits bounce through a clearing. They were white as snow, their ears flickering, and their pink noses jumping up and down as they ate whatever was left to find. They hopped away when Charlie accidentally stepped on a twig and crunched it.

"Dad!" Melissa scolded him, smiling.

"Sorry!" Charlie raised his hands.

Melissa's cheeks were bright pink from the chill. Sarah insisted they head back to the farmhouse to warm up. "After that, we have to go grocery shopping," she said. "That kitchen is too good to resist. I'm going to make a feast."

Back at the farmhouse, Sarah made a long list of groceries. She pestered Charlie to ask the owners if they could stay at the farmhouse a few days more rather than continue their road trip immediately.

"Wouldn't it be nice to pretend we live out here?" she said, curling her hair around her finger absently.

"You want to pretend to be the farmer's wife?" Charlie teased.

"I'll wake up at four in the morning to milk the cows," Sarah said. "And I'll collect all the eggs from the chickens."

Charlie stood behind her and wrapped his arms around her stomach. Together, they gazed through the window as the soft late-afternoon light blessed the fields. Within the hour, it would be inky black. It was time to go.

Sarah insisted on driving to the grocery store. Melissa sat in the passenger seat, flicking through the radio stations, as Charlie watched the trees from the back. It was rare that he was a passenger in his own car, and he enjoyed it.

At the grocery store, Sarah was authoritative, ordering Melissa and Charlie to put duck, eggs, potatoes, Brussels sprouts, and various ingredients for sauces in the cart. She added three bottles of dark red wine, a Malbec and two Primitivos, then winked and said, "I don't know if I want to leave that farmhouse ever again!" Charlie had a strange fantasy of living half-time in the farmhouse and half-time in Greenwich Village, allowing themselves the best of both worlds. Now that his career had taken off to the stratosphere, there wasn't a lot they couldn't afford.

And maybe Melissa would stay out east if they had the farmhouse. Maybe she would fall in love with the woods and the big, open sky.

When they left the grocery store, it was already dark.

Charlie insisted on driving. Sarah called him a control freak as she slipped the keys into his hand and winked. Melissa scrambled into the backseat and buckled her seatbelt. The drive back to the farmhouse was only fifteen minutes. Sarah spoke about the first steps of her cooking routine, asking Charlie and Melissa if they were ready to play their parts.

"You know me, Mom," Melissa joked. "I can't even make canned soup."

"And it's time to change that," Sarah insisted. "You're going to graduate in six months! Oh, Charlie. We've failed her as parents. She should know how to feed herself."

Charlie laughed. He whizzed them through dark forest roads, his lights flashing through the trees. Overhead, a full moon guided them, thick and yellow. Charlie felt completely at peace, his hands slipping along the steering wheel, his foot against the gas. He was imagining the night ahead of them— the conversations they would have over dinner, the movies they would watch. He imagined making love to Sarah that night, reminding her of the tremendous depths of his heart. He'd never loved anyone like her; he never would.

That's when it happened.

From the woods, three deer burst out in front of him. One of them was frightened by the oncoming lights and stalled, and Charlie slammed on his brakes. It was too late. Two of the deer smashed into his front window, and the car careened off the road and flipped. Charlie experienced the crashing sounds and the adrenaline of the car going through the air as though it were all a part of a game, as though he would be able to pause the accident and go back to "start" to do it again. His wife and daughter's screams joined the shattering glass. And then, there was only darkness. They were upside down at the edge of the road, far away from anything they knew or understood. Charlie was only semi-conscious; he couldn't make sense of anything. The rules of this new world had nothing to do with his previous one. And he knew he would never have love again.

Chapter Fourteen

Present Day

Charlotte couldn't describe herself as a business-minded woman. Rather, she'd committed herself to the arts at a young age (and to love, of course, which hadn't worked out), and she'd barely scraped together a living on her books— which wasn't exactly proof of business know-how. But throughout the days after she, Van, and Louise had cleaned up the inn, Charlotte got to thinking. Charlie had seen something here; he'd seen dollar signs. Perhaps Charlotte could draw that cashflow out herself without the meddling of a greedy Manhattan developer. Maybe all wasn't lost.

With the help of Google and a few library books, Charlotte set to work on making a business plan. As Van slept in her bedroom, she took her shifts with Ethan, jotting notes to herself and staying up later than she should have. "Burning the candle at both ends," Louise suggested when she came over in the morning to see Ethan. "Don't tire yourself out too much."

But Charlotte felt renewed with purpose. When she had a sufficient strategy set up for the next five years, she decided to approach Grandpa Hank to ask for his go-ahead. The inn was his, after all. And she expected him to be all in.

Grandpa Hank put on his glasses and read her business proposal quietly, his brow furrowed. Throughout, Charlotte sat across from him at the kitchen table, held her breath, and clasped her hands. She hoped her grandfather felt her tremendous love for the old place. She hoped he understood this was an act of honor.

When Grandpa Hank raised his eyes to look at her, they echoed his fatigue. "Thank you for this, Charlotte," he began quietly.

Charlotte's heart thumped. "I really think, if I apply for a grant from the state, we can get this place up and running by next Christmas," she scrambled to say. "I don't know if you read the part about New Jersey's commitment to historic properties. It behooves them to ensure places like the Cherry Inn stay active."

Charlotte was impressed with herself. She wasn't sure she'd ever said the word "behooves" before.

Her grandfather's eyes reflected his emotion. He removed his glasses and spoke gently, staring at the table between them. "Ten years ago, after we stopped taking guests, I probably would have jumped at a business proposal like this. I was heartbroken about giving this place up. And I suppose that's why I've continued to cling to it over the years, living in the apartment attached to it like some kind of ghost."

Charlotte swallowed the lump in her throat. This wasn't how she'd envisioned this conversation.

"It was your grandmother's dream to open this place,"

Grandpa Hank went on. "But your grandmother has been gone a long time. And I don't think she'd want to leave us with all this stress."

Charlotte blinked back tears. She racked her brain for something to say, anything to convince him. But Grandpa Hank suddenly looked very old and tired. He stood from the kitchen and rapped his knuckles on her business proposal, which she now felt resembled a children's project.

"I'm going to take a nap," he said. "I sleep almost as much as the little one these days."

In Van's bedroom, Ethan wailed with hunger. From the kitchen, Charlotte listened to Van's soft murmurings as she nursed him. Charlotte stood, shivering with sorrow, slotted her arms through her coat, and stepped through the drafty inn to get to Main Street. When she hit the sidewalk, she stormed toward the diner, urged on by a power she didn't understand. She was on the brink of tears, but she didn't want to give in to them.

Louise was in her diner outfit, helping a customer pay his bill. One of the twenty-somethings she'd hired whipped through tables, carrying platters of food. It wasn't as busy as it had been lately, a lull between lunch and dinner, and Charlotte collapsed in a booth and placed her chin on her fist. Louise appeared with a cup of coffee and a piece of rhubarb crumble. Her eyes weren't as hard as they'd been when Charlotte had first come to White Plains.

"I showed him the business proposal," Charlotte said.

"I guess it didn't go well?"

Charlotte sipped her coffee. "I'm trying to think of other ways to convince him."

"You think you and I are stubborn? Wait till you see how stubborn your grandfather can get," Louise said.

"It's genetic," Charlotte said with a wry laugh.

Louise tapped her shoulder gently. "Let's just have a good, final Christmas at the inn. All of the Summers, together again. After that, we can figure out how to sell the place and move on with our lives. What do you say?"

Charlotte was touched by how kind her mother seemed. It took her all the way back to her childhood when she'd considered her mother to be a goddess. She'd slept beside her in bed night after night, amazed at how wonderful she'd smelled, like lilacs and vanilla. She'd dreamed of becoming just like her.

Louise hadn't mentioned any kind of romance with Bert yet. Charlotte prayed Louise would tell her when the time was right. She prayed their love was strong enough to build a future upon.

After Charlotte ate her pie and drank her cup of coffee, she hugged her mother goodbye and wandered back through town. She felt strange and nostalgic, as though her heart was a balloon apt to float out of her mouth and into the sky. She was so out of her mind, in fact, that when Charlie Bryant appeared on the sidewalk in front of her, she hardly recognized him; she took him to be yet another guy from the city, here to experience the "magic" of small-town life. He waved her down.

"Charlotte! Hey."

Charlotte blinked at his handsome, happy face. Was it possible he was actually pleased to see her? She'd assumed she was just another woman in an endless stream of women, that he was a typical Manhattanite who wined and dined women and then abandoned them. After dinner at the Italian restaurant, he'd texted her a few times, but she'd more or less written him off, deciding that her "attraction" to him was something she needed to ignore. He would be gone from her life by the end of the year. It was best to get that out of the way. It was best to take control.

"Oh. Hi, Charlie." Charlotte tried not to smile, but his was so infectious that she had to match it. Against her will, her heart pounded. "What are you up to?"

"I just discovered something extraordinary," Charlie said. "Would you like to see?"

Charlotte hadn't expected this, either. "Are you just walking through White Plains, looking for someone to kidnap?"

"I promise, it's worth it," Charlie told her. "Come on."

What could Charlotte do? She sidled up beside him, inhaling the smell of him— wood-burning fireplace, the woods, the snow. He didn't smell like a Manhattanite. There was none of the overpowering cologne or expensive fabric.

To Charlotte's surprise, Charlie led her to the Presbyterian Church.

"I just popped in here on a walk," Charlie said as he opened the door. "And I couldn't believe the architecture. It's truly sensational."

Charlotte probably could have drawn what the Presbyterian Church looked like without ever entering its doors again. After all, she'd spent endless Sundays in its pews, drawing on her bulletins, waiting for the pastor to finish his sermon. She'd even been married there and had both of her babies baptized by the pastor working at the time. Her mother had attended both baptisms, but she'd sat in the back, her face scrunched.

"It's rare to find architecture like this in the city,"

Katie Winters

Charlie was saying, his arms stretched out in a dramatic gesture toward the ceiling. "I mean, this is pre-1850s. You can tell by the rafters. And the stained-glass windows are sensational! I asked one of the women working in the office if she knew when those were put in, and she said they're originals from 1813. Charlotte, can you imagine?" Charlie shook his head. "In Manhattan, I'm surrounded by so much new. I'm in charge of developing a lot of it. Yet here, surrounded by history? I feel humbled."

Charlotte was speechless. For a long time, she listened as he went on about what he loved so much about this church.

"I guarantee that the people who come here every week don't know how special it is," Charlie said. "I'm thinking about coming on Sunday, just to tell them."

"They would love that," Charlotte said, uttering her first words in a while. "The people who go to this church love this church deep in their bones."

"Then they deserve to know."

Charlotte swallowed. Drawn to his energy, she stepped toward him and crossed her arms over her chest. "I used to come here every Sunday."

Charlie's eyes lit up.

Charlotte pointed toward the side door near the pulpit. "For a few years, I came in and out of that door to play the piano," she went on. "I was terrible, but the congregation loved it. They gushed about my skills afterward."

"Do you still play?"

"No. And trust me, that's a blessing for everyone." Charlotte laughed. She realized she was standing less than a foot from Charlie, locked in his gaze. "I've never seen the church the way you're seeing it. I always took it for granted."

"It's not your fault," Charlie said. "That's just the nature of being human."

"I wish I could fix that about myself," Charlotte breathed. "I wish I could remember to be grateful for everything before it goes away."

Charlie looked on the verge of tears. Charlotte hadn't expected to see him like that, not ever. She considered making an excuse and fleeing the church. If she stayed much longer, she would do something she would come to regret.

"I was married in this church," Charlotte said softly.

Charlie smiled.

"That was a disaster," Charlotte went on.

"Don't blame the architecture," Charlie said.

"I won't." Charlotte crossed her arms over her chest. When she glanced beyond Charlie at the front of the church, she could half-imagine herself and her ex-husband kissing for the first time as husband and wife. They were like ghosts.

"Can we get out of here?" Charlotte asked.

Charlie and Charlotte walked side-by-side down the aisle and burst back into the glittering sunshine of that frigid December afternoon. As they descended the front steps, Charlotte reached out to take Charlie's hand. It was warm and huge in her small, chilly one. When he turned to look at her, his eyes told her what she already knew.

There was something between them. Something real. And perhaps Charlotte was too tired to deny it any longer.

All at once, his lips were upon hers. His arms

wrapped around her, and he placed his hands on her lower back, swallowing her with his warmth. His kiss was tender, not too long. When it broke, Charlotte bit down on her lower lip. She didn't want to smile. She didn't want him to know how much it meant to her.

The snowfall had thickened, and it filled Charlie's hair. Charlotte didn't step away from his embrace.

"I couldn't kiss you in the church," Charlotte said softly.

"The last time didn't turn out so well," Charlie affirmed. "I get it."

Charlotte laughed, surprised, as ever, with his sense of humor. "I didn't know rich Manhattanites were so funny."

"We're not," Charlie said. "But I wasn't always a rich Manhattanite."

"They let you keep some of your Midwestern sense of humor."

"In exchange for my soul," Charlie agreed. "Exactly."

Charlotte stumbled down one of the church steps. She felt out of her mind. "Thank you for showing me the church." She said it formally, as though they'd just had a business meeting. She stepped further away from him, forcing herself from their dream.

"Where are you headed?" Charlie asked.

"I have to help Van," Charlotte lied. She was suddenly overwhelmed with terror.

"Grandmother duties."

Charlotte walked away from him, leaving him there on the church steps. At the corner, she waved goodbye, and he smiled, his dimples deep, the winter winds whipping through his hair. If only she'd met and married someone like him, she thought now, before completely dismissing the memory. Charlie was just a fling. Yet another confusion in what was turning out to be the strangest Christmas season of all. She couldn't give her feelings too much power.

Chapter Fifteen

C harlie watched Charlotte walk quickly away
from the Presbyterian Church. His lips still
held the memory of hers, of their soft warmth,
and he ached to run after her and draw her into his arms
again. Something glimmered in her eyes. Was it fear?

Charlie wasn't sure what to do with himself. He
shoved his hands in his pockets, turned on his heel, and
walked through downtown, tugging at his hair, killing
time. It was never far from his mind that the accident that
had taken both Sarah and Melissa from him had
happened approximately ten miles from the downtown of
White Plains. Although they'd been buried in Manhattan, he felt closer to them here, as though their spirits
echoed through the woods and fields. Even standing in
the Presbyterian Church, enthralled with the architecture, he'd known how much Sarah would have appreciated it, too. She was never far from his mind.

Charlie returned to the woods, walking slowly as the
light dimmed over the treetops. It had been three years
since the accident— three years in this world alone.

Charlie recognized how grim he'd become. He'd lost his enthusiasm for everything. He wanted to run away from being himself. That had been the whole point of coming out here. Yet, of course, the guilt got into every emotion, poisoning it. Even now, as he fluttered with feelings for Charlotte Summers, his stomach twisted with it. He couldn't love anyone but Sarah. He had to uphold her memory above everything for the rest of his days.

It was far worse to think about Melissa. She'd been at the dawn of her life, eyes widening as university approached. There was no telling the good she could have done in the world, the joy she would have brought to her friends, family, and future romantic partners. She would have been a brilliant mother if she'd decided on that. And she would have made Sarah and Charlie proud.

Charlie reached the cabin and stumbled at the doorway. His heartbeat was loud in his ears. Inside, he made another fire and poured himself a glass of whiskey. Perhaps he could go to bed early tonight. Perhaps, in that way, he could escape his swirling thoughts.

His phone rang. It was Baxter. Charlie ignored it, deciding he'd call him back tomorrow. But after three missed calls, Timothy texted Charlie to say:

> TIMOTHY: Just pick up the phone, Charlie. Baxter isn't the kind of guy you yank around.

Charlie rolled his eyes into the back of his head. He felt like a puppet.

"Evening," Charlie said as he answered the phone.

"There he is!" Baxter called. "My man. What kept you? Are you out in that forest of yours, hunting for bears?"

Charlie laughed falsely and stared into the fire. "What can I help you with, Baxter?"

"I just wanted to check in about our new project," Baxter said. "I've told so many people about it. Little White Plains, New Jersey! Who would have ever thought we'd stake our claim there?"

Charlie blinked several times, trying to rid his mind's eye of Charlotte's gorgeous face. Their kiss had done a number on him.

"You've convinced the family to sell, haven't you?" Baxter asked.

"I'm still working on it," Charlie said.

"Small-town folks are about as stubborn as they come," Baxter agreed. "Do everything in your power to push them out of there."

"I will."

"You're the great Charlie Bryant," Baxter assured him. "Nothing can get in your way."

After the call, Charlie made himself a sandwich and considered what to do. His initial plan, which was to get to know Charlotte, pretend to be her friend, and then convince her to sell the inn, now seemed dead in the water. If he brought it up, that glimmer in her eyes would fade immediately. She'd see him as a cruel and manipulative Manhattanite— which was exactly the persona Charlie was trying to escape.

But what if he didn't convince the Summers to sell? What would Baxter do with him? Would he see it as proof Charlie had lost his edge and abandon him?

He supposed that wasn't the worst thing in the world. But then again, if Charlie Bryant wasn't Charlie Bryant, the sought-after developer, then who was he? Down to his bones, he was a sad widower. He was the man who'd killed his wife and only child in a horrible accident. He was evil.

Late that night, Charlie pulled up his text message conversation with Charlotte and stared at it, trying to decipher what they were to one another. They'd had some banter; they'd made some jokes. Charlie had even sent a photograph of himself in the woods, with a cardinal planted on the branch behind him, along with the caption: **"Look! I made a friend."** He'd felt so foolish the moment he'd sent it off. But Charlotte had responded with a heart emoji. What did that mean?

As Charlie stared at his phone, aching to write her something, to remind her of the beautiful moment they'd shared, he received a text. It was from Charlotte. It felt as though she'd been staring at their text exchange, too, yearning for the same things.

> CHARLOTTE: I never thought I'd see the Presbyterian Church like that.

> CHARLOTTE: I'm wondering what else you can introduce to me in my own hometown.

Charlie's heart banged against his ribs. He was suddenly and very painfully aware that when he'd done all his pre-marriage dating, cell phones and texting hadn't been a part of the equation. What could he say? He was terrible at this.

> CHARLIE: I'm falling in love with the details of this little town. That's for sure.

Charlie winced. He'd used the word "love," which was probably too earnest.

CHARLOTTE: It's strange. I've hardly thought about Manhattan at all since Van and I got here. It's like I completely abandoned my old life.

CHARLIE: I know what you mean. Now that I'm living the life of a hermit, I don't know how I'll ever go back to the Upper West Side.

CHARLOTTE: Maybe we can make the occasional trip to the city to get bagels.

CHARLIE: Ha! You're right. That's the one thing I miss.

CHARLOTTE: Have you been to Heaven's Hot Bagels on the Lower East Side?

CHARLIE: Best bagel in the city!

CHARLOTTE: Right?!

Charlie was grinning from ear to ear, staring down into the bright light of the phone. He felt as though Charlotte was right in front of him; he could hear her voice in his head.

CHARLOTTE: This probably sounds crazy. But would you like to go to the Christmas tree farm with me tomorrow? I invited all of my cousins to the Cherry Inn for Christmas (for one last celebration before we decide what to do with the old place). And we need a Christmas tree desperately.

* * *

Charlie woke up early the next morning, did fifty push-ups on the floor by the fire, drank two cups of coffee, and got ready to meet Charlotte. The plan was to meet at the Christmas tree farm, take the tree back to the inn, set it up, and maybe grab lunch afterward. As Charlie walked through the woods, he watched the sunlight sparkling through the trees and across the heaps of snow, and he reminded himself to be grateful for all of it— for the sky and the wind and the animals. "Remember to live in the moment," Sarah had said so often. "Remember to count your blessings."

Charlie arrived ten minutes early to the Christmas tree farm and waited awkwardly by the entrance. A pick-up truck appeared down the end of the gravel road and crept toward him, and the driver waved, smiling. It was Charlotte.

"Whose truck is this?" Charlie asked with a laugh as she rolled open the front window.

"My grandpa's," Charlotte said. "He doesn't know we're getting the tree."

"You stole it from him?"

"He's taking a nap," Charlotte offered. "He'll never know."

Charlotte parked the truck in the lot and joined Charlie at the edge of the adorable Christmas tree forest. A man in a lumberjack coat approached and told them to select any trees from a particular section; the ones toward the back weren't big enough yet. They were saving them for next year.

Charlie and Charlotte roamed through the trees

quietly, sometimes catching one another's gaze. Their boots crunched through the snow.

"I love that smell," Charlotte said finally, pausing in the very center of the Christmas tree farm. "I've noticed you smell like that a little bit. Probably from your life in the woods."

Charlie's heart thumped. Charlotte was less than a foot away, and they were five minutes from the entrance of the Christmas tree forest, shrouded in shadows. If he wanted to, he could kiss her again, here beneath the cerulean sky. A bird flashed overhead, cawing.

Before he chickened out, he cleared the distance between them and kissed her. She responded to him, cupping her lips around his and drawing her arms around his waist. Charlie felt outside of time. It was as though every decision he'd made since the party at the new apartment building had brought him here.

Suddenly, there was the sound of giggling children. Charlie and Charlotte jumped away from each other just as three kids between the ages of eight and eleven scampered past them. Charlotte's cheeks were pink with embarrassment.

"Why do I feel like we just got caught doing something wrong?" Charlotte whispered.

"It's like we're in high school, sneaking off between classes," Charlie agreed, smiling.

They held hands after that, gliding through the aisles of trees. It took them much longer than most others to find the "perfect" tree. Charlie's theory was that they wanted to extend the experience as long as they could. They wanted to steal another several kisses, swaddled in the scent of pine trees, lost in the dream they were building.

Charlie and the lumberjack from earlier secured the

tree to the truck as Charlotte paid. When Charlotte returned, she did a double-take with the lumberjack and said, "Wait! Aren't you Craig?"

The lumberjack laughed. "I wondered if I knew you. Charlotte Summers, right? Gosh, it's been ages."

They hugged, and Charlie felt an inexplicable wave of jealousy and nausea. Charlotte was telling Craig that she'd invited her entire family to the Cherry Inn for Christmas. She wanted to uphold her childhood memories and remind her grandfather of how magical the inn truly was.

"Watching the inn fall apart has been tragic," Craig affirmed. "I'm glad you're here to bring some life back to the old place."

Charlotte beamed as she said goodbye and scrambled into the truck. Charlie waved to the lumberjack and got in beside her. The lumberjack peered at him curiously.

"You know him from high school?" Charlie asked, hating the way his voice wavered.

"I had a big crush on him in middle school," Charlotte said.

"He looked at you like he was in love with you."

Charlotte glanced at Charlie with surprise. Had she realized Charlie was slightly jealous? Did she have the upper hand?

Suddenly, Charlotte's phone rang. Charlie put it on speakerphone, allowing Charlotte to focus on the road.

There was the sound of a baby screaming. Charlie's stomach twisted. It drew him all the way back to 2004 when he and Sarah had brought Melissa home. She'd been a sickly baby for a little while, falling asleep for no more than forty-five minutes at a time and then crying again. Charlie and Sarah had joked they'd aged ten years in just a few months. At the same time, they'd never been happier.

"Mom?" Van's voice came over the speaker. "Ethan won't stop crying." She sounded like she was on the verge of tears, too.

"We're on our way back to the inn," Charlotte announced. "Seven minutes. Okay?"

After Van hung up, Charlotte winced. "I hope it's okay that I help Van for a little while?"

"Of course."

Charlotte smiled. "You don't give off the vibe of being a baby lover."

Charlie raised his shoulders. What vibe did he give off, exactly?

"Babies are okay," Charlie said. This was the biggest lie he'd ever told.

"But my grandson is extraordinary," Charlotte assured him. "I'm sure no grandmother has ever said that before."

Charlotte pulled into the back lot of the Cherry Inn and led Charlie into the back entrance of the apartment. Ethan's cries were the only sound, and they got louder and louder as they approached, becoming like a nail through their eardrums as they entered. Van was in the kitchen with baby Ethan, who was red as a tomato, his cheeks shining from his tears. Van looked on the brink of a nervous breakdown. Grandpa Hank was standing in the kitchen, looking worried.

"Louise had just left," Grandpa Hank said. "If only she would have stayed a little bit longer."

Charlotte hurried toward Van and took Ethan in her arms. Charlie crossed his arms over his chest and stood awkwardly in the corner. Van and Hank peered at him curiously.

For a little while, Charlotte did everything she could think of. She tried, again, to feed him; she rocked him gently and massaged his stomach. All the while, Charlie shifted uncomfortably, his mind awash with memories. Melissa. She'd been just as small as Ethan; she'd been so helpless; she'd brought him so much joy.

And then, suddenly, he heard himself speak. "Do you mind if I give it a try?"

Charlotte gaped at him. But after nearly twenty minutes of trying to calm him down, she shrugged and handed Ethan over gently. Instinct took over. Charlie held Ethan's head; he cradled him. His heart shattered. Ethan waved his tiny fists with rage and sorrow.

Slowly, Charlie knelt on the ground and placed Ethan on his baby blanket. He could feel Van, Charlotte, and Hank watching him intently. Probably, it was just as confusing to them why they'd trusted him. Then, Charlie took Ethan's feet in his large hands and began to cycle his legs as though he were on the tiniest bicycle in the world. Ethan hiccupped with surprise. And slowly, slowly, the tension in his face released. His crying petered out.

"It was gas," Charlotte whispered. "Just ordinary gas."

"How did you learn to do that?" Van asked.

Charlie scooped Ethan back into his arms. His cheeks were cold and wet. Had he been crying? As he passed Ethan to Van, he recognized that familiar urge again. He needed to get out of there. He needed to run.

"I'd better get on the road," he said.

"What? No!" Charlotte laughed nervously. "We just got here. We have to put up the tree."

But handling little Ethan like that had torn Charlie up inside. He couldn't make sense of it. Melissa's very short life had begun to flash before his eyes: her first steps, her first piano recital, her first soccer game. He'd swelled with pride at each of her accomplishments. *"That's my baby girl,"* he'd said. *"That's my Melissa."*

"I'll see you soon," Charlie assured Charlotte, although he wasn't sure he could take it. He was a broken man.

Before Charlotte could say another word, Charlie rushed out the door and crunched through the yard, headed back to the cabin. It was just past noon, and the sun was directly overhead. Downtown rooftops shimmered in a way that made Charlie feel like he walked through a dream. It was hard to believe anything in his life would ever feel normal again.

Chapter Sixteen

Charlie walked for hours. He returned to the cabin, made a fire, and then let the fire burn out. He felt twitchy and unable to calm himself down, wrapped up in memories of Melissa and Sarah. When he found himself again in front of Rudy's bar, he could do nothing but march inside, sit down, and ask for a Dark and Stormy. Rudy said, "Coming right up."

Up above, the bar's televisions showed several local sporting events, Christmas specials, and news stations. Charlie watched a children's Christmas choir performing, their mouths opening and closing silently as the television was on mute. Melissa had been in a choir, as well, often practicing her soprano wherever they went. She'd insisted on performing for the bagel seller, the hot dog stand, and the bodega clerk. "She doesn't have a bone of shame in her body," Sarah had commented. "I wish she could teach me to be like that."

"How's it going?" Rudy interrupted Charlie's reverie. "You've been here a little while now, haven't you?"

"More than two weeks," Charlie said. "Hard to believe."

"And how are you liking it?"

Charlie took a long sip of his drink. On the one hand, he'd come to the bar so that he didn't feel so alone. On the other, he wasn't sure he had the energy for these kinds of conversations.

"It's nice," Charlie offered with a shrug.

Rudy looked mildly disappointed. "I've seen you around town a little bit with my cousin, Charlotte. I guess you met the first time here at the bar?"

Charlie nodded and blinked, not wanting to betray any emotions. "I wanted to help her flip the Cherry Inn," he reminded Rudy. "But she hated my designs. I thought she was going to rip them up."

Rudy laughed. Charlie was surprised to hear laughter bubbling from his own throat.

"She's stubborn," Rudy affirmed. "We grew up together and used to argue all the time about silly stuff. Even if she was obviously wrong about something, she held her ground for as long as she could. She could have argued the sky was purple for hours. By the end of it, she would have believed it completely."

Charlie loved that about Charlotte. He sipped his drink, cursing himself for using the word "love," even just in his mind.

"She's had a hard go of it," Rudy went on, drying a pint glass and shelving it. "That husband of hers was a real piece of work. The first time I met him, I said something to Charlotte like, 'Really? This guy?' But I could tell that made her angry, so I immediately made a joke out of it. Pretended that I really liked him."

Charlie tilted his head. "What was he like?"

"He was very handsome, of course," Rudy went on. "He was creative and arrogant. He thought he had a mastery of everything. But one thing that sticks out to me is how overtly he insulted Charlotte the first time he met the family."

Charlie's eyes widened.

"You know, she writes and illustrates her own children's books?"

Charlie hadn't known that. His heart thudded. He found that incredibly beautiful and suddenly longed to hold one of her books in his hands, to flip through its pages and indulge in the gorgeous details.

"Anyway, her ex insinuated that she wasn't writing 'real' books. That children's books required less intellect than adult books. It was really rude and cruel," Rudy went on. "You could see he was trying to belittle her to feel better about himself. At that time, though, Charlotte was already pregnant with Van and head-over-heels in love."

Charlie couldn't believe Rudy was spilling this story so easily. It was almost as though he needed Charlie to understand Charlotte on another level, to recognize that he handled delicate, breakable goods.

"But my Aunt Louise hated him," Rudy said. "I don't know the details, but she told Charlotte she was making a huge mistake. They didn't speak after that. Even after Van and Collin were born, Louise kept her distance."

"That Summers' stubbornness," Charlie said.

"Exactly." Rudy sighed. "But when I heard Charlotte and Louise were hanging around each other again— and that Charlotte had made a new friend in you— I felt so hopeful. Maybe this is the year the curse is broken."

Charlie was quiet for a moment. Rudy looked at him,

captivated, as though expecting him to say something that would solve the Summers' problems.

"You heard about Charlotte inviting all us cousins to the Cherry Inn?" Rudy went on.

Charlie nodded. "She's calling it one last Christmas. But I can't imagine her parting with the Cherry Inn."

"No way," Rudy said. "If I had money to bet, I'd say we'll be celebrating at the Cherry Inn every year for the next twenty."

Charlie smiled. It was comforting, thinking of that family all together, year after year. He imagined Charlotte at the helm, roasting turkeys, baking pies, and turning into her Grandma Dee.

"I don't know how she'll manage it," Rudy added. "But if anyone can, it's our Charlotte."

Charlie finished his drink and stared into the glass. Rudy was directly on the other side of the counter, staring at him.

"And maybe you'll be around for Christmas?" Rudy broached.

Charlie forced his eyes toward Rudy's. The bar was completely empty except for the two of them, and another snowfall peppered the dark air outside.

"White Plains wasn't a random decision," Charlie said finally. "I came here for a reason."

Rudy set his jaw. "You wanted to buy the inn and flip it?"

"No. I couldn't care less about developing anything right now," Charlie said. He rubbed his chest. "Three years ago, my wife, daughter, and I rented a farmhouse on the outskirts of White Plains."

Immediately, Rudy's face paled with recognition. "You're that father."

Charlie's heart thudded. His story had probably spread like wildfire through these parts. Accidents around Christmastime were always particularly heartbreaking—and memorable.

"Your wife and daughter," Rudy whispered. "I'm so sorry."

Charlie raised his shoulders. The word "sorry" no longer affected him. "I haven't properly mourned," he said finally. "I threw myself into work and pretended like they never existed at all. I became a monster, someone I didn't recognize. And now, here I am, just about ten miles from where I killed them..."

Rudy waved his hand. "It was an accident, Charlie."

Charlie swallowed the lump in his throat. Shame pressed hard on his shoulders and chest. He removed his wallet and paid Rudy, adding a huge tip. There was a reason he never spoke about Sarah and Melissa aloud. Talking about it made it so much more real and present.

"I'd better be on my way," Charlie said, unable to look at Rudy.

"Stay for another, Charlie. On the house."

But Charlie was already at the door. The bell jangled as he re-entered the darkness, and he slipped back into the night toward the woods. He couldn't believe he'd revealed himself like this. Before long, Rudy would probably spread his secret across town— and Charlie would be forced to find a cabin elsewhere. He couldn't take being known.

Chapter Seventeen

Very late on the night after Charlie had fled the inn, Charlotte got up the nerve to text him.

> CHARLOTTE: Thank you again for your help today! Little Ethan is happy and sleeping.

> CHARLOTTE: Would you like to come over this week to help decorate? We found boxes upon boxes of decorations in the attic. Most of them belonged to my Grandma Dee— and even Grandma Dee's mother.

> CHARLOTTE: You'd be paid handsomely with Christmas cookies, of course.

It took Charlie more than an hour to answer back. Throughout, Charlotte drank tea and checked her phone anxiously. The house around her felt very still, with Van, Ethan, and Grandpa Hank sleeping deeply.

CHARLIE: I have a few work responsibilities to take care of this week.

CHARLIE: I'll probably go back to the city right after Christmas.

CHARLIE: Maybe we can grab a coffee before I go.

CHARLIE: Glad to hear about Ethan.

The tone was stunted and strained. It took Charlotte's breath away. Just to make sure, she scrolled up to their previous texting conversations, where she found them bantering playfully. Dare she say it, they'd been flirting! And now, Charlie acted as though they'd met once, briefly, and owed one another nothing.

Where was the romance they'd been building? Why had it suddenly died?

Charlotte lay like a starfish on her bed, which was the same mattress her mother had slept on as a teenager. It needed to be updated, and it had begun to give Charlotte a backache.

There had been no sign of her and Charlie's "flirtation" dying— until the moment Charlie had taken Ethan in his arms and stopped him from crying. He'd handled the baby expertly, so much so that it was clear he was a father. But why hadn't he ever mentioned his children?

Charlotte was broken-hearted and confused. The night was sleepless, and she eventually gave up around four-thirty to feed Ethan and clean the kitchen. By six, she was in the inn, building a fire in the fireplace, grateful for its warmth and its friendly crackling. The Christmas tree she and Charlie had picked out was in the corner, just as thick and tall as she remembered it being as a child. Aloud, she said, "It's perfect." But after that, it felt as though there were stones in her stomach. She'd wanted to share the decorating with Charlie. She'd wanted to show him the Cherry Inn's Christmas magic.

Suddenly, the door between the apartment and the inn opened. Van appeared with little Ethan strapped to her chest.

"There you are!" Van smiled and entered, leading Louise in after her.

"What's all this?" Louise asked her hands on her hips. "When did you get a tree?" She looked like she wasn't sure if she was angry or happy about it.

"I'd love your help decorating," Charlotte said softly. "Some of the cousins will be here as early as the 20th. Collin is flying in on the 21st if you can believe it."

"Collin's leaving California for Christmas?" Louise touched her chest.

"I couldn't believe it, either," Charlotte said. "But it means we've got our work cut out for us."

It was time to put their heads down and focus. Van set up a Bluetooth speaker to play Christmas classics— "White Christmas," "Silver Bells," and "Have Yourself a Merry Little Christmas," as Charlotte and Louise opened the first Christmas boxes. Immediately, Louise's face was illuminated with memories of her mother, Grandma Dee. She handled each ornament with care, telling Charlotte stories about each one. "This one broke when I was ten or eleven," Louise said of a tiny wooden sled, a snowman riding it. "But Dad glued it back together for us." Another ornament was a framed photograph of Louise, her siblings, and her mother and father. Louise was eight or nine in the photo, sporting a bob haircut that made her face look like the moon. "What a horrible picture of me!" Louise said with a laugh. Charlotte's eyes were misty.

Yes, she'd wanted Charlie's help decorating. She'd wanted to feel his strong arms around her again, to steal kisses throughout the morning. But decorating with Louise and Van was much, much better. It was the tender care the inn needed.

Around noon, the three of them took a break and returned to the apartment to make tomato soup and grilled ham and cheese sandwiches. Grandpa Hank was awake and rosy-cheeked, and he ate with them at the kitchen table before admitting he wanted to take a crack at decorating the Cherry Inn, too.

"I can't let you three do this all by yourselves," he said.

Charlotte was euphoric. As she placed Christmas decorations around the main room, she watched as her grandfather and mother pawed through the remaining decorations, reciting memories to one another. If Charlotte tricked her mind, she could half-imagine Grandma Dee in the next room, baking Christmas cookies.

The next few days found a similar rhythm. Now that so many cousins were returning to the Cherry Inn for Christmas festivities, every single guest suite in the Victorian house needed to be prepared. Charlotte delegated tasks and made frequent trips to the nearest store, purchasing new sheets, lamps, robes, soap, and lotions. After the first room was finished— the one with the green wallpaper— she and Van assessed it from the doorway and said, "It doesn't look half-bad." It definitely needed new wallpaper, and the floors needed to be polished. But all in all, it would do.

"I hate to admit it," Charlotte whispered, "but doing all this makes me believe in the inn again. Maybe we could open it ourselves, after all."

Van's smile was crooked. "And never go back to the city?"

"Never again," Charlotte said. "Would you be willing to do that?"

Since their escape from New York, Van had hardly mentioned Grant. Grant hadn't reached out about his son. It was as though he'd never existed at all. Charlotte searched for that sorrow in her daughter's eyes— but it was as though her love for Ethan had eliminated that.

"I've already been dreaming about it," Van offered.

"Grandpa doesn't want us to," Charlotte said.

"Maybe Grandpa doesn't know what he wants," Van said.

"Does anyone?"

* * *

Charlotte's cousins, siblings Bethany and Steve, along with Steve's wife and Bethany's husband, arrived on the evening of the 20th. Charlotte was breathless with expectation, fearful that her cousins would immediately point out all that was wrong with the old place. But instead, Bethany and Steve threw their arms around Charlotte and gushed about how gorgeous the Cherry Inn looked— both on the inside and outside. This felt like confirmation of something. Charlotte was headed in the right direction.

"That tree is spectacular," Bethany said. "It looks just like it did in my memories."

"The house needs a lot of work," Charlotte offered, tilting her head.

"Does it?" Bethany glanced around at the living room, which was tinged orange from the roaring fire. Van returned from the apartment with a big platter of Christmas cookies, urging Bethany and Steve to sit down. "Maybe a paint job here and there? But I can't imagine anything much more than that. It needs to stay entrenched in the past." Bethany's eyes glinted with nostalgia. "I hate that I haven't been back in years."

"Me too," Charlotte whispered. "Am I crazy for wanting to take over this place?"

Bethany squeezed Charlotte's arm. "It would be crazier to let this place go."

Grandpa Hank, Bethany and her husband, Steve and his wife, Charlotte, and Van gathered around the fire that night, bubbling with expectation for the days ahead. Already, they were cultivating a plan about which cookies to bake (lemon bars, cut-outs, buckeyes, cinnamon rolls, peanut clusters, and many more), which Christmas movies to watch, and whether there would be enough snow to make a snowman outside. Memories were tossed from one side of the room to the other, with Bethany and Steve adding to Charlotte's memories when hers failed.

"My favorite Christmas was when I was ten or eleven," Bethany said. "I came downstairs before everyone else and found the tree lit up and all the presents untouched and glowing. To me, it felt as though Santa had literally just left. I curled up on the couch and fell asleep again, and when I woke up, I was surrounded by family members. Someone handed me a big plate of cinnamon rolls. It was heaven. Oh, and I'm pretty sure Mom and Dad got me a bike that year. I ran that thing ragged until I got too big for it."

Charlotte smiled, remembering when they'd discovered a sleeping Bethany on the couch, all curled up, too excited about the morning to remain in bed.

The front door of the Cherry Inn opened, and a sharp draft of chilly air came through the living room.

"Mom?" Charlotte jumped to her feet to greet Louise, who'd said she would come by as soon as she closed the diner.

Louise was very pale. She remained in the foyer with her black peacoat on, waving timidly at the newcomers. "Good to see you all. Charlotte, can I speak to you for a moment?"

Charlotte frowned and hurried into the foyer, where they stepped off to the side to avoid the rest of the family's eyes. Louise tugged at her gloves nervously.

"Are you okay, Mom?" Charlotte asked.

Louise rolled her shoulders back. "I need to tell you something."

"Okay?" Charlotte's heartbeat felt urgent, and she struggled to draw air.

"At the diner this evening, there were two men from the city," Louise said. "They were richer than rich. Those faces that just immediately make you feel like you're nothing compared to them, you know?" Louise's nose twitched. "And they had all these papers in front of them. Business proposals. Spreadsheets with very big numbers."

Charlotte had no idea where her mother was going with this.

"I eavesdropped on them for a while," Louise offered. "And they were talking about your friend. Charlie Bryant. They said he was in the process of securing the purchase of the Cherry Inn. They said that Charlie was 'changing the mind of the family.'" Louise flapped her fingers with air quotes. "And they even said something about the Summers family being 'small-town idiots' who don't know how to make a buck." Louise glowered.

Charlotte was speechless.

"Finally, I butted in," Louise went on, "and asked them about their plans. They said they want to transform the place into a spa?" Louise rubbed her temples. "I barely held my tongue."

"I mean," Charlotte stuttered, "Charlie initially wanted something like that, too. But he understands we won't sell. I've told him. It's in the past."

"According to these men, Charlie is trying to manipulate us," Louise said. "As though we're easily manipulated! As though we're not the most stubborn people around!"

Charlotte felt the edges of her heart crack.

"How else do you explain these men being at the diner?" Louise demanded. "They're like vultures, waiting for the Cherry Inn to die. And Charlie was the one who brought them here. Think about it, honey. When was the last time you even saw Charlie?"

Charlotte wanted to lie. She wanted to tell her mother that she saw Charlie all the time, that he hadn't abandoned her right when she was beginning to trust him. But Louise recognized something in her eyes; she saw the pain.

"Oh, honey," Louise breathed. "We always get ourselves wrapped up with the wrong men, don't we?"

Charlotte bristled. All at once, she was twenty years old again, listening to her mother belittle her and her life choices. How could it be happening? She'd thought she was smarter. She'd thought she'd overcome her past.

"Mom?" Charlotte's voice cracked. "Why don't you want me to be happy, huh?"

Louise's face fell. "That's not what I said."

"You see how painful this is for me," Charlotte said, "and you poke and poke at that pain until it gets so much worse. Why do you do it?" Her voice rose. It was probable that everyone in the living room could hear, but she didn't care.

Louise flared her nostrils. "I won't be spoken to like this."

"Fine," Charlotte said. "You're not wanted here tonight."

Louise glared at her and said, "Fantastic. I have places to be." She turned on her heel and bolted back into the night. Charlotte remained in the foyer with her palm on the door. The wind rushed against the old house and made the door rattle, and her body quaked with fear. None of this made sense.

"Mom?" Van entered the foyer, her face marred with worry. "Did Grandma leave?"

Charlotte nodded. "She has to work early tomorrow." The lie came out easily. She knew, even as she said it, that Van wouldn't believe it.

Van collected Charlotte in her arms and held her. Charlotte let out a single sob, marveling at how wonderful it was to be held by her own daughter. Van was a mother, now— and she knew the comfort that emanated from her body, from her heart.

"It's going to be okay," Van whispered. "We're here together in the Cherry Inn. We're safe."

Chapter Eighteen

I t was late, nearly midnight, and Charlie was wide awake, still dressed in his jeans and a flannel, feeding the fire. It was the 20th, just five days till Christmas, and he hadn't spoken to Charlotte in what felt like ages. The loneliness that came with missing her was heavy on his shoulders, and he'd begun to neglect himself — not trimming his beard, showering only every other day. The only person he had any sort of communication with was Rudy, Charlotte's cousin— who'd stopped by twice since their heart-to-heart. "I'm here for you, man," he'd said as they'd sat by the fire together. "I can't imagine what you've been through. But I don't want you to think you're alone."

His thoughts filled with Charlotte. Charlie pulled up their last text exchange from five days ago— when he'd caved and allowed himself to say hello, even when he'd already told her he probably couldn't see her anymore. He was weak.

Their last exchange looked like this:

CHARLOTTE: I'm going to pull out my Grandma Dee's chocolate orange cookie recipe in time for Christmas. But be warned: they're going to stop you in your tracks. Your entire life will be different afterward. Some people who taste these particular cookies go insane because they don't know how they ever went without them.

CHARLIE: Haha. Those sound like dangerous cookies.

CHARLOTTE: I'm sorry to change your life like this.

CHARLIE: Maybe my life needs to be changed.

CHARLOTTE: About that...

CHARLOTTE: I'm sorry if I came on too strong.

CHARLOTTE: I haven't dated in a really long time. I probably don't really know how.

CHARLOTTE: Not that we were dating. I don't know what that was.

Charlie had taken a full ten minutes to respond. During that time, he'd felt Charlotte buzzing with anxiety all the way back at the Cherry Inn. She'd put herself out there, over and over again, and Charlie had been forth and back, never fully there and never fully gone. He was her Christmas ghost. And he hated himself for it.

What he'd answered with was this:

CHARLIE: Don't worry about it.

Don't worry about it. What did that mean? If she hated him, now, he understood. He'd proven himself to be lower than scum in the dating pool.

He'd spoken briefly to Rudy about this, telling him that he just wasn't sure he was capable of loving anyone again— certainly not someone as wonderful as Charlotte. Rudy had said, "You're worthy of love, you know. Even if you don't know how to accept it." To this, Charlie had said, "It doesn't feel like I deserve anything. Not after what I did."

He was forty-nine years old. But in many ways, he'd died three years ago, out on that country road with his wife and daughter.

There was a knock at the door. Charlie stood swiftly, his adrenaline spiking. He checked his phone to see if Rudy had texted about coming over. The bar closed at eleven tonight; it was possible he'd decided to drive by and say hello.

But when Charlie opened the door, he discovered Baxter Bailey and another man, similarly moneyed, in a suit jacket, a white t-shirt, and a pair of dark jeans. They were drunk, their cheeks red, and they smiled at Charlie like leering teenagers. Charlie checked to see Baxter's driver had been the one to bring them. He couldn't stand drunk drivers.

"Charlie, my boy!" Baxter leaped forward to hug him. "This is Dean Winston, my associate."

"Hello?" Charlie backed into his cabin and closed the door behind them. Dean and Baxter surveyed the single room as though it was a cage at the zoo.

"It's even better than you described it," Dean said to Baxter, as though Charlie wasn't there. "Downright adorable."

"Charlie," Baxter said, turning to catch his eye. "We've been scouring White Plains all day."

"Up and down the streets," Dean said. "Eating at as many establishments as we could."

"And we've decided the Cherry Inn is just the beginning," Baxter said.

"We've fallen in love," Dean said. "And we want to make it a destination Christmas town."

"Picture it," Baxter continued. "Every quaint inn is just as luxurious as your plans for the Cherry Inn. Every restaurant is just as rustic as the ones they have— but with Michelin-star chefs. People will come from far and wide to enjoy the 'traditions' of this Christmas village."

"But we'll make up the traditions as we go along," Dean affirmed. "Based on what's selling at the moment."

"It's perfect," Baxter babbled. "I'm so thrilled you discovered this little place, Charlie. I was getting so bored in Manhattan."

Dean and Baxter smiled at him, showing too many of their very white teeth. Charlie remembered Timothy first forcing him to get his teeth bleached; it had hurt like heck, even though everyone had said it wasn't supposed to.

"I want to see the plans, Charlie!" Dean rubbed his palms together. "Baxter has been talking about them all day. But I want to see the real deal."

"We almost stormed into the Cherry Inn today," Baxter said excitedly. "Just to see what it's really like in there. But we saw a very old man on the front porch, gazing out into the distance."

"He looked tragic," Dean said, as though it were a joke.

"So, we decided to wait till after the sale goes through," Baxter agreed.

Charlie sat back down by the fire. His thoughts were tying themselves into knots. Baxter and Dean grabbed his bottle of scotch and poured them each a glass, ready to bring Charlie into their celebration. But when Dean handed Charlie a glass, Charlie felt so outside of his body that he nearly dropped it.

"To our future!" Dean cried.

"To White Plains!" Baxter said.

Charlie didn't drink with them. He stared into the fire for a long time as the pressure in his chest grew. All he could think about was Charlotte, talking about her gorgeous memories in the Cherry Inn or about the way she'd looked in the Presbyterian Church, captivated by the rafters and the stained glass. There was a purity to her love of the world, one that was completely alien to Baxter and Dean.

And Charlie would have no part in whatever terror they wanted to create here in White Plains.

"You can't have the plans," Charlie said, mostly to the fire.

"What was that?" Baxter still sounded celebratory.

Charlie stood up and faced them. He was reminded of fraternity brothers he'd met in passing a long time ago, all of whom had come from money and planned to drink themselves silly through college. Afterward, they were given whatever job they pleased. The world was their oyster. And Charlie had dismissed them as idiots. How had he gotten himself so involved with them?

"I said, I won't give you the plans for the Cherry Inn. The Cherry Inn is not for sale. And White Plains folks won't accept any money you throw at them. This place isn't Manhattan. Your money isn't as powerful here."

Baxter's smile had fallen. Dean shifted his weight and looked back and forth from Charlie to Baxter.

"I'm sure you're kidding," Baxter said.

"I wouldn't joke about this," Charlie said. He then stepped toward the door and touched the handle. "I'd like to ask you to leave. Immediately."

Baxter raised his eyebrows. "Charlie, my boy. Don't you remember our history?"

"I don't care about that."

Baxter took a dramatic step toward him so that his nose was only a few inches from Charlie's. He practically spit on him as he said, "I built you, Charlie Bryant. You're nothing without me. The fact that I wanted to work with you on this was a gift I was giving you, not the other way around."

Charlie's jaw stiffened. "I've already asked you to leave, Baxter. Take your friend to whatever five-star hotel you found around here, and leave me alone."

Baxter looked smacked. Charlie wondered if anyone had ever stood up to him before. It seemed unlikely.

"Very well," Baxter said. "Let's go, Dean." He stormed toward the door and bucked into the night, with Dean directly behind him. He looked like a baby chicken following her mother. As drunk as they were, they left the door wide open and then jumped into Baxter's car. The wheels squealed as they cut from the driveway and into the night. Charlie closed the door quietly, his head ringing.

"That's it," he muttered to no one. "That's the end of that story."

But even as he said it, he knew Baxter Bailey was the sort of man who sought revenge. Charlie just wasn't sure when he would strike.

174

Chapter Nineteen

Four days before Christmas, a navy blue rental car pulled up outside the Cherry Inn. Charlotte flung from the front door and threw herself onto her son, Collin, who'd brought her granddaughters, Brinlee and Elisa, all the way across the continent for their first Christmas in the Cherry Inn. It was almost too much to bear, seeing their little faces in the backseat, so different than they'd been more than eight months ago, the last time Charlotte had seen them.

Charlotte stepped back, her hands still on Collin's shoulders, and took stock of him. Now that he was twenty-six, he looked completely like a man. He'd lost his baby cheeks, and he had a full beard. The little boy who'd held her hand when they crossed the street in the city was no more.

"Hi, Mom," Collin said.

"I can't tell you how happy I am that you're here," Charlotte said, hating how earnest she sounded.

"Grandma!" Elisa and Brinlee burst from the rental

car and hugged her legs. Charlotte felt doubled over with love for them.

"My girls!" she cried, waving hello to her daughter-in-law, Quinn, as she walked around the front of the car. "Let me show you the inn. You're going to love it."

Inside, Charlotte's heart broke again when Van and her brother hugged tightly, and Van introduced Ethan to his uncle. Ethan was now nearly four weeks old, and he kept his eyes open a little bit more every day, staring up at Collin as though he understood their connection immediately.

"Van, he's gorgeous," Collin breathed, shaking his head. Privately, he'd once told Charlotte that he didn't think Van would ever have children since she was dating "that horrible guy." He'd wanted to be an uncle so badly. He'd gotten his wish.

"How has it been?" Quinn asked. "The first one is an adjustment."

Van laughed. "He sleeps almost constantly! But wakes up every hour or so for a few minutes, needing me. I'm more in love than I've ever been, but I haven't entered REM sleep in what feels like ages. I feel insane."

"That sounds about right," Quinn said.

"Mom's been a huge help," Van said, then added, "And Grandma."

"Oh! Is Grandma here?" Collin eyed Charlotte nervously. He knew all about Charlotte and Louise's multi-decade feud.

Van shook her head and gave Collin a look that meant she would explain everything later. Charlotte's stomach flipped. Her and Louise's argument last night had re-opened old wounds. Maybe they'd never fully healed in the first place.

Charlotte showed Collin's family their suite upstairs, with its queen-sized bed and two trundle beds for Brinlee and Elisa. The girls were overjoyed with the inn, running through the halls, their dresses flying out behind them, just as Charlotte and her cousins once had. They were amazed by the library, with its mighty shelves, its thickly bound travel books and encyclopedia, and the maps hanging on every wall, and they begged to crawl into the attic, where, they presumed, a mystical creature was lurking. The Cherry Inn was always rife with stories. After just thirty minutes, Brinlee and Elisa had fallen into its fairy tale spell.

"When was the last time we came here?" Collin asked Van. "Must have been a summer fifteen or sixteen years ago?"

"Something like that," Van agreed.

"Never at Christmas," Collin said. "It was a great idea to bring everyone together again, Mom. Thank you."

Charlotte floated back downstairs to check on dinner, which she'd been hard at work on for the past three hours. By nightfall, all the cousins, children, and spouses of the Summers family would be at the inn— and they'd be hungry. She imagined them seated in the dining room of the inn, candles flickering on tables, conversations a dull roar punctuated with spurts of laughter. She imagined hours of communion as a balm to heal their past.

Charlotte still had her work cut out for her. Van breezed in and out of the kitchen to check on her, dice garlic, stir potatoes, or give Charlotte a report about who else had arrived.

"I haven't even met all of these people," Van said as she placed Ethan back in his bassinet. "But they all have

Summers family features. One of them, your cousin Frankie, looks so much like me!"

Charlotte hadn't seen Frankie in more than twenty years. She gripped a wooden spoon and considered Frankie, remembering her wide forehead, and intense eyes. But a moment later, Frankie appeared in the kitchen itself, revealing herself to be Van's gorgeous, older twin. Frankie scooped Charlotte into a hug and said, "There she is! Our brilliant children's writer!"

Charlotte blushed. "Didn't you hear? I might be an innkeeper instead."

"Here? At the Cherry Inn?" Frankie's jaw dropped. "Oh, Charlotte. Wouldn't that be a dream?"

"You should move back to White Plains to help out!" Van suggested.

Frankie gave a wry laugh. "I don't think I have the temperament for hospitality. Besides, I've traded in my New Jersey identity for an Oregon one. I don't think I could give it up."

"You always have a home here," Charlotte assured her. "Just in case."

Frankie crossed her arms over her chest and leaned on the counter, turning her head to take in the kitchen, the adjoining living room, and the photographs of their grandma and grandpa. Her breath quickened.

"It's like I'm ten again," Frankie said. "I feel like Grandma is going to come out of her bedroom and insist we help her bake cookies."

"I felt like that when we first arrived," Charlotte said meekly. "But gradually, the apartment transformed into a little home for us."

Van nodded. "It's the first home my son has ever known."

Frankie toyed with her necklace, her eyes still on their grandma and grandpa's bedroom door. It was as though she felt if she stared at it long enough, she could return them to the past and bring their grandmother home.

The bedroom door burst open, and Grandpa Hank stepped into the shadows of the hall, wearing a sleepy smile.

"Grandpa!" Frankie rushed around the counter and charged into a hug. She had all the energy of her child-hood self.

"My darling Frankie," Grandpa Hank breathed, holding her close.

"Grandpa, it's so good to be back," Frankie said. "All the way here, I was dreaming about your Christmas Eve story."

Grandpa Hank winced and closed his eyes. It occurred to Charlotte that telling that story was like poking his old wounds over and over again; it was a reminder of the tremendous love he'd lost.

"It was always so magical to hear it," Frankie hurried to add. "That's all."

Charlotte poured Grandpa a glass of water and placed it on the counter, watching Grandpa Hank as he walked slowly toward the kitchen. His skin was gray, and the circles beneath his eyes were heavier than ever. It was as though he hadn't slept in days, even though Charlotte had been sure he'd been napping.

"Grandpa? Are you all right?" Charlotte's voice wavered.

Grandpa Hank drank his water and set the glass back down with a loud clack. "I have to tell you something, Charlotte. Before it goes on any longer."

Charlotte's stomach twisted. "Okay?"

"This morning, I went for a walk with my friend Mike," Grandpa Hank went on, "and I was approached by two men from the city. They asked to buy me a cup of coffee to talk something over. I'm a friendly man. I knew they weren't accustomed to White Plains, and I wanted to show them a good time. We stopped by the diner; Louise wasn't working. And it was there that they outlined their plan to flip the Cherry Inn into something truly sensational. Something luxurious. Something that could make everyone a whole lot of money."

Grandpa Hank wet his lips. Charlotte remained speechless.

"The number they wrote down was astronomical," Grandpa Hank said. "It's the kind of money that would change the rest of my life. It's the kind of money that could send my great-grandchildren to prestigious universities. We could take family vacations together somewhere spectacular. There are so many places I never went to, Charlotte, because I was always needed here at the inn. The Cherry Inn was my life's work— but it took and it took from me. It took my time and my health and my money."

Charlotte's eyes filled with tears. She recognized the fear in her grandfather's eyes. It was never easy to tell your family the truth.

"Of course, thinking about some city folks ripping up the inside of the Cherry Inn has me upset," Grandpa Hank went on. "Your grandmother and I refurbished so much of this place. It's our blood, sweat, and tears. But the only necessary thing in life is change. And I believe these men coming to town and offering me this opportunity is God himself, telling me it's time to move on."

Charlotte wanted to cry out, to tell him this wasn't

God. This was materialism. This was capitalism. This was the quest of very rich men to make even more money than they'd had before. They were never satiated. There was never enough.

For a moment, Van, Charlotte, and Frankie held the silence. Grandpa Hank looked as though he was confessing something horrific, as though he'd just committed a crime.

"Have you already signed something?" Frankie asked quietly. "Is the deal finalized?"

"No," Grandpa Hank said. "I told them I needed to talk to my family first. But I also told them I was pretty sure I'd go through with it."

Frankie gestured vaguely toward Charlotte. "You know that Charlotte wanted to take over the inn? To build it back up again?"

Grandpa Hank's eyes glinted with tears. "I know," he whispered. "But Charlotte, you don't want this life. You're living a beautiful life in the city. You're writing all those gorgeous children's books. I don't want you to strap yourself to a sinking ship."

Grandpa Hank looked even more exhausted. He palmed the back of his neck and excused himself back to his bedroom. "I have some more thinking to do," he muttered.

"I hope you'll join us for dinner?" Charlotte's voice broke.

Grandpa Hank turned back to lock eyes with her. "I'll be there, Charlotte. Thank you for making our final Christmas in the Cherry Inn so special. I'll never forget it. And neither will the rest of the family."

After Grandpa Hank disappeared behind his bedroom door, Charlotte scrubbed at the bottom of the pot of mashed potatoes with a wooden spoon, swirling with anger and sorrow. She couldn't believe these men had gone out of their way to stalk her grandfather and manipulate him.

Then again, was it manipulation? If the money was as good as her grandfather said, and her grandfather really wanted that money, who was Charlotte to say he shouldn't take it? He was the owner of the Cherry Inn, after all.

Had Charlie been one of the men? Or had they been the men Louise had reported seeing at the diner, vultures stalking their prey? Charlotte closed her eyes and wavered from foot to foot, suddenly dizzy.

"What are you thinking, Mom?" Van asked.

Charlotte sighed. "I'm thinking that I need to go see your grandmother. Can you handle the food for a little while?"

Chapter Twenty

L ouise wasn't at her house, nor was she at the diner. Charlotte rushed through downtown White Plains with her heart in her throat, her cheeks frozen with tears. She called Louise three times, but Louise either ignored the calls or didn't notice them. Where was she?

The thought struck Charlotte just before she gave up: Louise had a lover.

Charlotte tore up the steps of Bert's house and steeled herself before she rang the bell. She heard the television behind the door, along with the murmur of two different voices. Bert cracked open the door and smiled at Charlotte immediately; his eyes were guarded. He knew about the newest feud.

"Is my mother here, Bert?"

"She is." Bert scratched his beard. "I can't promise she'll come to the door."

"Can you tell her it's extremely important?" Charlotte said, her breath heavy with fog.

Bert beckoned Charlotte into the foyer and closed the

door behind her. The foyer was decorated with signage that indicated Bert loved fishing more than anything else in the world. A stack of old newspapers sat in the corner, and a framed photograph of Bert and a young man hung on the wall. Was that his son?

Louise appeared in the doorway between the foyer and the kitchen and glowered at Charlotte with more vitriol than she'd ever shown— impressive, given their history. "Can I help you?"

Charlotte let her shoulders drop. She hated showing such weakness in front of her mother. But wasn't showing weakness one of the main elements of loving and being loved? Wasn't that part of the game?

"I'm really sorry, Mom." Charlotte stuttered. "I'm sorry I dismissed you last night."

Louise's face softened. "Oh no," she breathed. "Don't tell me it happened."

"They tracked down Grandpa. The offer was enormous, obviously. Just as you said it would be. And Grandpa is considering it."

"That makes sense." Louise's face was marred with pain. "My father has been through a lot. It doesn't surprise me that he wants to leave the past behind."

Charlotte's lips quivered. "And I know it's selfish of me, coming back after so many years away and demanding that he keep the inn. I just felt so ready for it. A new phase. A new identity as an innkeeper." She swallowed the lump in her throat. "I'm so tired of struggling in the city. I'm tired of fighting with my publishers and having my ideas for children's books rejected."

Louise took several steps into the foyer and touched Charlotte's elbow gently. Her eyes were nothing but compassionate.

"Most of all, I'm tired of sleeping alone," Charlotte whispered. "And I'm tired of picking the wrong men. Men who are clearly only out to ruin my life."

Louise nodded, her eyes to the ground. "I hate that Charlie didn't turn out to be who you thought."

"The thing is, he's exactly what I originally thought he was," Charlotte said with a wry laugh. "I shouldn't be surprised. I should have trusted my gut."

Louise closed her eyes and stepped further toward Charlotte, drawing her into her arms. Charlotte nestled in her warmth, feeling the soft beating of her heart through her sweater. "I'm just so sorry, Mom," Charlotte whispered. And this time, she wasn't sure what she was apologizing for. Perhaps it was for all of it, for their decades apart. She never wanted that to happen again. Why had they been so arrogant, thinking they had an unlimited amount of time on Earth?

Charlotte wiped her cheeks with the sleeve of her shirt. "You and Bert have to come to the inn tonight," she said, trying to clear her throat. "I've been cooking up a storm all day. All the cousins are there. And my granddaughters, Elisa and Brinlee."

Louise smiled immediately. "You've got to stop manipulating me with my great-grandchildren," she said. "I just can't stay away."

Bert agreed to join the party. As he donned his coat, he glanced at Louise, checking on her emotionally, making sure she was all right after the intense conversation. Louise squeezed his hand and said, "You're going to love the Cherry Inn at Christmas, Bert. I'm so glad you can join us."

The three of them walked slowly back through downtown, engaging with the Christmas lights and the sparkling stars in the black sky. Bert announced he felt like the luckiest man in the world, being escorted through town by two such beautiful ladies. Louise burrowed against him and said, "You're so sappy, Bert."

It was a surprise to the entire Summers clan when Charlotte led Louise into the foyer of the Cherry Inn. All eight cousins, spouses, children, and grandchildren were in the living room or dining room, drinking wine, eating cookies, feeding the crackling fire, and catching up. Bethany jumped to her feet and cried, "Aunt Louise is here!" And one after another, the cousins filtered into the foyer to swallow her with hugs and draw her deeper into the party. Bert was introduced, and he clapped everyone on the back and said, "What a spectacular inn! What a wonderful Christmas!"

At eight, the Summers gathered around dining room tables for the feast. Charlotte was seated between Van and Grandpa Hank at a table with Louise, Bert, Collin, Quinn, Brinlee, and Elisa. Charlotte, Frankie, Van, and Louise took turns bringing the meal into the dining room: enormous platters of turkey, ham, roasted pumpkin with feta and onion, cheesy potatoes, candied yams, Brussels sprouts, a mysterious Jell-O dish that one of the cousins had made, homemade rolls, and numerous salads, their dressing glinting in the soft candlelight. And when everyone had a full plate and a glass of wine, beer, juice, or water in front of them, Charlotte stood up, raised her hands, and said, "Will everyone join me in prayer?"

Charlotte closed her eyes and held Van and Grandpa Hank's hands. Because the dining room was filled to the gills with Summers family members, the silence around her seemed impossible. Everyone awaited her prayer.

"Dear Lord," Charlotte began, no longer versed in the

art of prayer, "I want to thank you for bringing the entire Summers family together after so many years apart. I want to thank you for our gorgeous memories here at the Cherry Inn and the tremendous love our Grandpa Hank and Grandma Dee always showed us. I want to thank you for our final year of Christmas here at the Cherry Inn before we move on to other memories and other plans. I'd like to ask for your continued blessings as we celebrate the next several days together. Our family love is an unbreakable bond that you've given us. We thank you, Oh Lord. Amen."

"Amen," the family murmured.

Hours later, after the pie was eaten, the plates were cleared and washed, and the kitchen was scrubbed to a shine, Charlotte found herself before the warmth of the fire, surrounded by her cousins. Rudy clapped the couch cushion beside him and said, "Saved you a seat, cuz."

Charlotte hopped onto the couch beside him and placed her head on his shoulder. Rudy was the closest to her in age and had always been her favorite. A long time ago, he'd been married, but they hadn't had children, and the romance hadn't worked out. Sometimes, Charlotte ached for what she perceived as his loneliness. But what did she know? Maybe he was the happiest of them all.

"What was it you were saying," Rudy asked quietly, "about this being our last Christmas at the Cherry Inn?"

Charlotte raised her head. Most of the cousins had overheard the question and turned their attention to her. They looked almost accusatory.

"Grandpa's selling," Frankie answered for her.

"He hasn't signed the papers yet," Charlotte hurried to add. "But yeah. Some very rich men want to flip the inn."

The cousins held the silence. With the fire crackling before them and the Christmas tree aglow in the corner, it seemed impossible this was anything but 1983. It seemed impossible these anonymous city folks would rip through the inn, through the fabric of their memories.

"I just hate it," Bethany whispered.

Everyone murmured their agreement.

"But Grandpa has to do what he needs to do," Rudy said. "And we have to respect that."

Not long afterward, the cousins returned to separate conversations, discussing their homes across the United States, how White Plains had changed, how they felt about parenting, their take on American politics— everything. Charlotte remained quiet, watching the flames.

And then, she heard herself say: "Do you remember that guy I met at the bar a few weeks ago? The developer guy."

Rudy flinched. "Charlie?"

"Yeah." Charlotte swallowed the lump in her throat. "I feel like such a fool for falling for him. It's so obvious he was just here to stake out properties."

Rudy arched his eyebrow but remained quiet.

"I mean, we only kissed a few times," Charlotte added, her cheeks burning. "But I was caught up in the whirlwind of that. He seemed so smart. So earnest. You should have heard the way he talked about the church down the road. I felt as though I was finally seeing the world through somebody else's eyes, and I liked what I saw."

Rudy grimaced and rubbed his neck. He looked nervous.

"I was so wrong about him," Charlotte went on. "I hate that I can't trust my instincts at all anymore. What will I do when I get back to the city? Just hole up in that apartment. Never date again. Oh, and what will I do about Van and Ethan? They can't go back to Brooklyn." She chewed on her lower lip.

"I don't think you were necessarily wrong about Charlie," Rudy said tentatively.

Charlotte furrowed her brow. "What do you mean?"

"There are things about Charlie you don't know," Rudy said. "Something horrible happened to him. Something that makes him dismiss the world."

"How do you know all this?"

"He told me," Rudy said. "I work in a bar. I'm basically the town therapist."

"And I guess you won't tell me what happened," Charlotte said.

Rudy shook his head. "All I can say is this. I think Charlie saw you as his first link back to 'real life.' Back to feeling like a normal man. But he got scared. Anyone would have in his position."

Charlotte gaped at Rudy. "He says he's going back to the city."

"I can't imagine that will happen," Rudy said. "I imagine him getting in that Porsche of his and driving out onto the open road. But I can't imagine he'll find what he's looking for. I don't even think he knows what he's looking for."

Charlotte's heart felt pulpy and bruised. "What should I do? He won't answer my text messages. He won't answer my calls."

Rudy raised his shoulders. His face reflected Charlotte's deepest fear: that it was too late. The window had closed. And Charlotte had to find a way to live with that, somehow.

Chapter Twenty One

Two days before Christmas, Charlie received a final text message from Baxter Bailey.

BAXTER BAILEY: We're going ahead with the sale without you. Thanks for nothing.

Only minutes after that, Timothy texted him. He'd found another job, another developer to assist. Charlie found himself in the strange position of getting everything he'd wanted. Timothy was off his back, and Baxter was long gone. But his stomach churned with anxiety, knowing he'd brought Baxter's wrath upon the Cherry Inn in the first place. Whatever money Baxter planned to throw Hank Summers' way was surely nothing to scoff at. But money was tainted; it lacked the romance that emanated through White Plains. Perhaps the money would eventually snuff it out.

Charlie donned his winter coat and went for another long walk through the woods. He hadn't heard from Charlotte in a while, and he'd begun to think she was an apparition, something he'd made up to serve as a cushion between himself and the horror of the real world. Now that the Cherry Inn was being sold, perhaps Charlotte would return to the city. Perhaps one day, Charlie would see her walking in Manhattan. Perhaps they'd lock eyes with one another and then pass by. Or perhaps they wouldn't even notice one another at all.

Charlie walked back downtown, looped around Rudy's and Jeez, Louise, passed the courthouse and the elementary school. The sky was very blue, and sunlight made the snow drifts impossible to look at; they were so bright.

Charlie finally got up the nerve to pass by the Cherry Inn. Main Street was overwhelmed with parked vehicles, presumably all cousins and other Summers family members, and as Charlie drew closer, he realized the entire Cherry Inn was humming with life. Speakers inside played "Have Yourself a Merry Little Christmas," and children scampered through the snow outside, rolling it into balls to secure bases for children. Their parents helped and frequently returned to the porch to sip something out of mugs— coffee, tea, or even hot wine. Charlie's heart thudded as he looked a little too long at each of their faces, making out features he'd once seen on Charlotte's. If he'd played his cards right, he would have been up there on the porch with the Summers. He would have gotten everyone another round of mulled wine. He would have shown the two little girls nearest him the better way to roll the snow.

Oh, his heart ached at the way everything had fallen apart. He'd been so close to something real. And he'd destroyed it.

"Charlie?"

A familiar voice drifted from the far end of the porch. It was Rudy, his face bright red with a chill between the flaps of his fuzzy cap. He bucked down the staircase and approached, crunching through the snow. Charlie felt on display. The two little girls turned around to gape at him. Hadn't Charlotte said she had two little granddaughters from California?

"Merry Christmas, man," Rudy said, clapping him on the back.

"Merry Christmas." Charlie sniffed. "You have a full house?"

"It's about to burst," Rudy affirmed. "Never a dull moment. It's even crazier than it was when I was a kid."

Charlie tried to laugh. "Must be nice to have everyone back together."

Rudy set his jaw. He looked contemplative. "It is." He blinked. "Would you like to come in for a while?"

"I couldn't," Charlie stuttered. "I'm on my way somewhere, anyway."

"No, you're not," Rudy said.

Charlie was speechless at being called out like that.

"Listen, man," Rudy said under his breath, "you need to come clean to Charlotte about what happened."

Charlie's heart thudded.

"I talked to her the other night," Rudy went on, "and she's so broken up about you. I'm not saying you need to marry her or even date her! I just want her to know she didn't imagine what was happening between you two. And I want her to know you're actually a decent guy."

"I'm not a decent guy," Charlie pointed out. "I'm the furthest thing from one."

Rudy touched Charlie's shoulder. "That's the thing,

Charlie. You need to fight this self-hatred. You've built a prison around yourself. You don't deserve it."

Charlie's mouth felt very dry. "I didn't have anything to do with the sale of the Cherry Inn," he said suddenly.

Rudy raised his shoulders. "What do I care about the sale of this inn? It's just a place. I'd much prefer my cousin and my new friend were happy. I'd much prefer if my new friend found joy again."

The two little girls had built a terrible base for their snowmen. They ran around it, screeching excitedly. It seemed they'd never seen snow before.

"She's in the apartment in back," Rudy said. "Just go knock on the door. She'll answer."

Charlie could hardly breathe as he walked around the house. It felt like walking the plank. His thoughts spun circles, searching for the right words to say and how to say them. But by the time he reached the back apartment, he was dull with panic.

That's when he saw her through the window.

Beautiful Charlotte sat in the La-Z-Boy, giving baby Ethan a bottle. She was completely alone, her eyes rapt with love for her grandson, and she sang just loud enough for Charlie to hear through the glass. Her voice was soft and dreamy, echoing a nursery rhyme Charlie hadn't heard in many years. Ethan kicked his feet lightly, pleased to be in the arms of his grandmother.

Charlie felt sucker-punched with memories of Melissa. How she'd needed him. How he'd failed her.

But for reasons he would never understand, Charlie forced himself to the back door of the apartment and knocked. He felt frozen with fear. There was the soft tapping of feet, and then the door opened to reveal Charlotte with Ethan still in her arms. The smile she'd prepared, probably in thinking he was a family member, fell immediately. Maybe Rudy had been wrong. Maybe this was the worst possible thing to do.

"Charlie?" Charlotte searched his face. "What are you doing here?"

"Do you mind if I come in? Just for a second."

Charlotte beckoned for him to enter and shut the door. The baby bottle remained on the counter, still half-full, but Ethan had fallen asleep in Charlotte's arms. Charlotte draped Ethan in the bassinet. Again, Charlie was struck with a memory of Sarah putting Melissa down just like that— with such tenderness.

"I came to apologize," Charlie said. "And also tell you I haven't been fully honest with you."

Charlotte crossed her arms over her chest. Her gaze wasn't judgmental.

"Three years ago, I went on vacation," Charlie said. "My wife, daughter, and I rented a farmhouse on the outskirts of White Plains. One night, I was driving us back to the farmhouse. There was an accident."

Charlotte placed her hand over her mouth. Charlie stared at the floor.

"There is no reason in the world that a father should outlive his daughter," Charlie went on. "And there is no reason he should walk away from an accident like that without his wife."

Charlotte cleared the space between them and took his hand. Her eyes were two glinting pools. Her touch was almost too much for him; he felt sure he would burst into tears.

"I am so sorry that happened to you," Charlotte whispered.

Charlie let out a single sob. He dropped his forehead onto Charlotte's shoulder and quaked. It occurred to him, now, that he'd hardly cried after Sarah and Melissa's deaths. He'd considered it cowardly to sit in rooms alone, crying. He'd considered it pathetic, given his guilt.

"It was my fault," Charlie said.

"No," Charlotte said, her hand over the back of his head, rubbing his scalp. "It wasn't your fault, Charlie. It was an accident. A horrible accident. It never should have happened."

Charlie shook his head. He felt like Jell-O. Charlotte led him to the couch and sat him down. She then whisked to the adjoining kitchen to brew tea. Charlie focused on his breathing, watching little Ethan sleep in his bassinet.

"I remember it really well," he said, nodding toward Ethan. "How amazing it is to be so needed. To feel like you have this purpose in the world."

Charlotte returned with two steaming mugs of tea. "Having him around has helped me more than I even understand, I think. I've been floundering for years." She sat beside Charlie and placed their mugs on the coffee table. "When Van reached out to me to say she was in labor, I was all by myself on Thanksgiving. I felt like the loneliest person in the world." She chuckled sadly. "And that was only a month ago."

"And now, the Cherry Inn is bursting with your family," Charlie said. "You couldn't be alone if you tried."

Charlotte nodded. "I'm sure you've heard it's our final Christmas."

Charlie winced and removed his phone from his pocket to reveal the text message he'd received that afternoon from Baxter Bailey. Charlotte read it. She didn't look surprised. Perhaps, Charlie thought, in her heart of hearts, she'd already understood that Charlie didn't want to hurt her. He hoped so, anyway.

"I'm so sorry I brought them into your life," Charlie muttered.

Charlotte touched Charlie's shoulder. "My grandpa wants to move on. Maybe he's right. Maybe it's time."

Charlie chewed his lower lip, at a loss. He considered his future— the grim blocks of Manhattan, potentially getting back into developing as a way to pay rent. It all felt soulless.

And then, he remembered something— his bank account.

It was a funny thing to think of now, seated in the tiny living room of the apartment attached to the Cherry Inn. He felt miles away from where money mattered. And yet, this place would be forever altered because of the power of Baxter's money. But Charlie had money, too. Heaps of it. And he no longer wanted it anymore.

"I want to buy the Cherry Inn," Charlie said.

Charlotte's eyes swam with confusion. "What?"

"I want to buy it," Charlie said, "for whatever price Baxter was willing to pay. If your grandfather wants to move on and have a nice life, that's fine. But I want to own this place. I want to build it back up. And I want you to be by my side in bringing it into the twenty-first century. I'll throw all my old plans out the window— and we can plan what we do together."

Charlotte's chin quivered. For a long time, she didn't say anything. Charlie suspected he'd stepped on her toes yet again. That he'd upset her. She stood, then disappeared into the other room and returned with an illustrated children's book. It was called *A Fairy Tale*

Christmas. Its front cover was a gorgeous illustration of the Cherry Inn, but far bigger than it actually was, so that it looked more like a castle than a Victorian home. Around it were mountains and thick woods. Beneath the house, the author's name was written: Charlotte Summers.

"This was the first book I ever published," Charlotte said, handing it over to him. "The first few pages of illustrations capture what the inn looked like back when I was a child."

Charlie nodded as he studied each of the pages: the gleaming hardwood floors, crackling fire, sturdy mahogany front desk, grandfather clock, and old-world paintings.

"I want to bring this magic back to the old place," Charlotte whispered. "I want the guests who come through here to be able to feel what I felt when I was a girl."

Charlie understood what she meant. For the first time, in looking at the illustrations, he felt as though he fully dove through her memories and steeped in her nostalgia. It was gorgeous to have memories that mattered so much to you. He understood that more than most.

Finally, Charlie raised his head, took her hand in his, and said, "I promise, we'll make the inn look just like this. Your Christmas dreams will come true." His voice caught in his throat. "And mark my words. You'll have the entire Summers family back here at the inn next year to celebrate the holidays."

Charlotte leaped forward and wrapped her arms around him. Charlie was so overwhelmed that he nearly dropped the book. He couldn't believe it; telling the truth had actually worked in his favor. Acknowledging his feelings hadn't destroyed him. Charlotte was in his arms, shivering with tears, covering him with kisses. And for the first time in three years, he felt a path forming before him, one filled with light and hope. He would do everything in his power to stay on it.

Chapter Twenty Two

One Year Later

It was Christmas Eve again. As was tradition, Charlotte had closed reservations for the week surrounding Christmas, clearing the guest rooms of city folks and preparing the Cherry Inn for the entire Summers family. From the state-of-the-art kitchen of the inn, Charlotte stood quietly with a glass of merlot, listening to her enormous family in the living room and dining room, digesting after a gorgeous feast of roasted lamb. Charlotte, Van, and her mother, Louise, had worked tirelessly on the meal all morning and afternoon. And now, Charlotte felt a wonderful relief.

The kitchen door sprung open to reveal Louise carrying little Ethan, who was now one year old. He rubbed his eye sleepily with his fist and babbled and squawked happily. "It's time to give him a last bottle and take him to bed," Louise announced.

Louise doted on the little boy, nearly always insisting on being the one to change him or feed him during family functions. Van was grateful for the help— especially now. She'd met someone, a firefighter here in White Plains, who'd swept her off her feet during the summertime. Jeremy was here tonight, cozied up with Van in the living room, laughing with Collin and Quinn. Since Ethan's birth, Van hadn't heard from Grant once— and the divorce had been finalized via lawyers. It was almost as though he'd never existed at all.

"He loves his great-grandma," Charlotte said, playing with Ethan's curls.

Louise reached for a clean bottle on a high shelf and then eyed Charlotte curiously. Charlotte now remembered their long-standing fights as though they'd been parts of dreams. They hadn't bickered much at all since last Christmas.

"This place is really extraordinary, Charlotte," Louise said finally. "I don't know if I've said that enough."

The previous year had been difficult. After Charlie had cleared the sale of the Cherry Inn with Grandpa Hank, Grandpa Hank immediately took a vacation to Florida to visit a few friends he hadn't seen in decades. He'd stayed there until late spring, at which point Charlotte and Charlie were already deep in the chaos of the Cherry Inn's refurbishment. Charlie hadn't skimped on any details, not in the library, nor the upstairs sunroom, nor the kitchen, which now had enough counter space for a full cooking staff. After his return from Florida, Grandpa Hank walked slowly through the changing house, his eyes misting. When he'd returned downstairs, he'd hugged Charlotte and shaken Charlie's hand. "Your grandmother would have loved this," he said. "It's got all the old magic."

Charlotte and Charlie had re-opened the Cherry Inn

in late October. Because of Charlie's connections in the city, they'd been booked full since then, with city folks coming to enjoy the changing foliage and, later, the Christmas decorations. Due to Charlie's excellent organizational skills and Charlotte's creativity, they operated the inn like a tight ship but never hesitated to personalize someone's experience. On top of that, they'd hired a world-class chef for the kitchen, which nobody in White Plains complained about. Locals dined at the restaurant frequently, then sat by the fire in the living room to catch up with Charlotte or Charlie. "You've really brought magic back to White Plains," Louise had said once, watching people stream in and out. "People want to make their old homes look nicer again. They feel a sense of duty to the town."

Charlotte left Louise in the kitchen with baby Ethan and wandered through the living room. Grandpa Hank was seated with Bethany, reading Charlotte's first book, *A Fairy Tale Christmas*, pointing out the illustrations of Grandma Dee. "You're going to tell your story tonight, aren't you, Grandpa?" Bethany begged him. "We all need it."

Grandpa Hank's eyes sparkled. He planned to return to Florida in January— a tradition he'd chosen for himself and one he couldn't have afforded without the sale to Charlie. It had done him good.

"I'll do it," he told Bethany. "I just hope I remember it."

"You didn't forget," Bethany said.

"You're right," Grandpa Hank said. "I never could."

Charlotte spotted Charlie's shadow out on the front porch. He was leaning against the railing, gazing out at Main Street. Sometimes over the past year, she'd caught him like this, lost in thought. She knew he was thinking about Sarah and Melissa. In falling in love with Charlie, she'd learned to fall in love with both of them, too. They would always be a part of him.

"Hey, stranger." Charlotte came onto the front porch with two glasses of wine and handed one to Charlie. As he turned to look at her, he smiled, and Charlotte shivered with recognition. They were in love— but it was a different kind of love than she'd ever known. It was supportive. It was quiet. It nourished her soul.

Charlie took the glass of wine and kissed her, wrapping his arm around her waist to draw her closer. Charlotte was lost in his warmth, and her mind's eye filled with hundreds of images of the previous year. Not everyone got to fall in love during the refurbishment of their grandparents' inn. It was her own personal fairy tale.

"Grandpa Hank is going to tell his story soon," Charlotte said.

Charlie tapped his nose against hers. "I wonder when you'll tell your story."

"What do you mean?" Charlotte's heart swelled.

"The story of us," Charlie said. "Of how we found each other here in the fantastical land of White Plains. Of how we found a way to start over in our very own castle." He tilted his head toward the Cherry Inn.

Charlotte closed her eyes, overwhelmed with a wave of love for him. "That's the story I've been telling myself ever since I met you."

"Who says fairy tales aren't true?" Charlie kissed her again.

Charlie and Charlotte held one another on the front porch of the Cherry Inn as a sharp draft came down Main Street, peppered with snow. The Cherry Inn was all lit up, its eaves lined with Christmas lights and its windows aglow. The Summers family was back where they belonged, preparing their hearts for Christmas. And Charlotte knew that without Charlie, it would have never been possible. That was real love.

Coming Next in the Frosty Season Series

Pre Order Mistletoe & Mischief

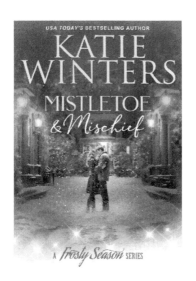

Other Books by Katie Winters

The Vineyard Sunset Series

Secrets of Mackinac Island Series

Sisters of Edgartown Series

A Katama Bay Series

A Mount Desert Island Series

A Nantucket Sunset Series

The Coleman Series

Connect with Katie Winters

Amazon
BookBub
Facebook
Newsletter

To receive exclusive updates from Katie Winters please
sign up to be on her Newsletter!
CLICK HERE TO SUBSCRIBE

Made in United States
Orlando, FL
17 December 2024

55999898R00117